Thorn In My Side

Mary Quinn

F&I

Published by
Fire and Ice
A Young Adult Imprint of Melange Books, LLC
White Bear Lake, MN 55110
www.fireandiceya.com

Thorn In My Side ~ Copyright © 2017 by Mary Quinn

ISBN: 978-1-68046-444-3

Cover Design by Caroline Andrus

To my family who suffered through late nights with me to write this and to my friends who helped me so much. I love you guys!

Chapter One

Once upon a time I used to love fairytales. It seemed like an easy way to live life: pick up a hot prince, and happily-ever-after just happened. Our town was magical, and I was a princess (in a way). Racheston, Massachusetts had a population of about 26,000 people (I didn't really pay attention to the last census) and my dad was the mayor; the king, if you will.

The streets were filled with pristine mansions that were so clean they sparkled on sunny days. But the older I got, the farther I moved away from the classic princess meets prince stories. The girls were dumb, the princes automatically assumed that any sleeping princess needed to be lip molested, and someone always wanted to ruin someone else's life. By the time I got to middle school most of those things were already happening, so why did I need to read about them? My mom lived for those fairytales. She didn't need to escape reality or dream of having the perfect imaginary life, because she already had it. She and my dad had already gone through the fictionally real romance. They had met and married at eighteen, then had me three years later. I even had an evil step-grandmother if you can believe that. But it took me a while to realize that not everything that glittered in Racheston was gold. Our town was dangerous, and each secret that was layered under the surface of the perfectly manicured lawns made it even more deadly. My family had a bigger part in this than I could have ever imagined, especially me. In this world of fairytales, the balance between reality and what lay in our shadows was precarious. All it would take to collapse our perfect lie was for someone to shine a light at the real Racheston.

Mary Quinn

Seven years ago

"Stop running around like that," my mom scolded in her delicately anxious lilt.

Why?" I whined, drawing out the word, continuing to circle the kitchen.

"Because it's not lady-like," she answered, her serene green eyes turning back to the bread she was kneading.

I skidded to a stop by our kitchen table, a reproachful pout on my face.

"What if I don't want to be a lady?" I asked, already knowing the answer. She turned around fully, leaning one perfectly manicured hand on the counter and placing the other one on her hip. Her eyes scanned my tie-dyed shirt, down my paint splattered jeans and rested on my ridiculously mud-splattered shoes. A crinkle formed between her eyebrows and her neatly symmetrical lips turned down at the corners. I was used to her disappointed looks by the time I was that age; it didn't even faze me. I started running around in figure eights while I awaited her answer.

"How will you ever get married if you won't act like a girl? Boys don't like slobs, Riley." Her unnaturally sweet voice left a bitter aftertaste in my mind, and I ran out of the kitchen crying. I hid under a pile of clothes in my closet until my dad came home from work and found me.

"She means well, Rye," he said, taking me into his arms. "She just wants you to be happy."

"Being married doesn't mean I'd be happy," I retorted, grumpier than I was mad at that point.

"It did for her, but we know it doesn't necessarily mean that you'll be happy being a housewife. Your mom knows that, just give her time to accept it," he replied and laughed, smoothing down my hair and kissing my forehead. "In the meantime, don't worry. Not all boys want a submissive wife. Someone's going to figure out how great you are and

2

sweep you off your feet."

"Who says that they're going to be the ones doing the sweeping?" I asked, sticking my tongue out at him, and wriggling out of his arms.

"True," my dad agreed, setting me down and standing up. "Now come on, your mom made dinner." We ate dinner as a happy family, and after clearing the dishes I went upstairs to my room to ignore everyone, (the warning signs of the angst-y teenager I was bound to become.) From where I sat on my bed I could hear my parents' voices as a low hum in my ears. Abruptly my dad's voice became harsher and louder; the loudest I had ever heard him been when talking to my mom. I leaned closer to my wall, pressing my ear against it. "It's her life!" I could hear him say. My mom's reply was too soft to hear through the plaster, but when my dad spoke again he sounded tired. "I know." My fifth grader mind soon wandered away from wondering what they had been discussing and soon I forgot it altogether. But I still took karate and self-defense classes all the way to high school to spite my lady-like mother after that day.

Chapter Two

Wasn't I a brilliantly feminist fifth grader?" I ask you, readers of this book. I assume that you're judging me because that's what society teaches you to do. If you didn't judge little fifth grade me then give yourself a pat on the back, but if I was correct then please stop reading after this sentence because guess what: I haven't actually changed. So stop... now.

Okay, that weeds out the people that I don't want reading my story. The rest of you get to hear the ridiculous but true story of my life. Wait, one more disclaimer: if you have a strong hatred of sarcasm then I'm a bad narrator to hear this story from. Ask my best friend Jessica to tell you; she was almost as close to the middle of this as I was. And she doesn't understand sarcasm so she'll be perfect for you guys. You can stop... here. The rest of you can't complain anymore after all of these warnings. Now you actually have to read the rest of this because you've made it this far. You're like a whole two chapters in, don't give up!

Now

I propped myself up with my elbow, keeping my eyes trained on the screen at the front of the room. The collar of my starched white shirt itched and I had to pull my plaid skirt down, yet again (the dangers of attending a prestigious private school with a uniform, part one). I scratched at the patch on my shirt that branded me as a student of Conlet

Academy as I felt my eyes starting to drift closed and snapped them back open. Then the teacher switched to the next slide on the French revolution and I could feel my eyes sliding closed again. You wouldn't think a brutal revolution using what surmounts to a giant knife on a wooden structure could be this boring. My teachers have talent. I heard another senior three seats behind me begin to snore. The juniors who hadn't caught senioritis yet shot disapproving looks in his general direction. I turned my head back to look at him. Jessica, who was sitting next to me, did the same and we exchanged exasperated glances. The third member of our little friend group was currently drooling on the desk along with the obnoxiously loud snores he was producing.

I wadded up an extra piece of paper and threw it at him, hitting him on top of the head. It had absolutely no effect on him; he continued to happily dream on. Our stereotypically old and stuffy teacher paused and narrowed his eyes at the back of the room.

"Lucas Moore, wake up," he wheezed, like he was talking through a cotton ball. One of the juniors sitting next to him poked him in the ribs and Lucas, or Luke as he was to everyone but dusty old teachers, woke with a start, his head shooting up.

"Present," he said in a bored voice and yawned. The girls surrounding him giggled and he winked at them in turn, a mischievous dimple appearing in his chiseled features. I rolled my eyes at him, making his flirtatious expression disappear to be replaced by a contrite smile.

"What are we going to do with him?" Jessica asked, after the bell had rung, with a maternal fondness.

"Save him from his admirers?" I suggested, surveying the mass of eyelash-batting girls surrounding him. "Do you think they know that doing that with their eyes makes them look possessed?"

"Poor girls." Jessica sighed. "They have no chance with you here." I flushed and glared at her.

"I don't know what you're talking about." I frowned. "We're just friends. Everyone knows that. It would be like dating my brother." But much, much better with less incest. I wasn't going to add that out loud though. She shook her head sadly at me and turned back to the mob of girls.

"Go get him," she said. "We're going to be late to English."

I pushed my way through the desks and girls and grabbed my completely overwhelmed friend by the wrist. "Come on," I said, tugging him towards the door. I could hear the disappointed sighs behind me.

"Thanks," he said, blinding me with his brilliant teeth.

"Put those away," I laughed as Jessica caught up with us.

"Better?" he asked, folding his lips over his teeth until he looked like an incredibly hot old person who had forgotten their dentures.

"Much." I nodded, turning into our English classroom. I narrowly avoided the leg that shot out to trip me, stumbling on my heeled combat boots. Luke caught me and held me upright as I regained my balance.

"Watch where you're going, Princess," Sterling Idels sniffed at me, claiming her front row seat.

"Watch your back, Idels," I snapped, straightening my uniform.

"Luke, did you hear that? She threatened me!" Sterling gasped, her (unfortunately for me) innocent looking hazel eyes, widening.

"From what I heard I think you deserved it," Luke replied, with a mocking pout. Sterling flushed angrily and glared at me. Jessica, unwilling to watch conflict, pushed past us to three empty seats in the back row. Luke tugged me along with him, sparing Sterling's face (for now) from my fist.

"Thanks," I grumbled, shaking Luke's hand off.

"Don't worry." He grinned. "I know you're not a princess."

"Yeah," Jessica agreed cheerfully, as always. "She's just mad that your dad beat her mom out for mayor again last week."

"Why Jessica," Luke frowned, winking sideways at me, "'beat him out' is not in your usual vocabulary of 'tra la la' and 'yay life'." She looked horrified at the insinuation of violence until she realized that he was kidding.

"Not nice," she said.

"God, Luke," I said, shaking my head disapprovingly but unable to hide my grin.

"You guys are both so mean to me." Jess sighed dramatically.

"It's tough love," Luke and I agreed simultaneously, after having this conversation hundreds of times. The teacher glanced at us to shut us up and class began. Luke doodled on my arm (nothing worse than smiley faces, thank god) while Jessica diligently took notes on the lesson and I stared blankly at the projector, pretending to pay attention. Half way through the speech on sentence structure, I gave up completely on even fake listening and stared blatantly at the clock. Luke was drawing a comic of two guys eating a pie on the inside of my arm. I giggled as the pen tip tickled the fold of my elbow and my teacher glanced up from her notes to glare at us.

"Riley Owens, is there something you'd like to share with the class?"

"If there was I would have said it louder, thanks," I answered, with a smile.

The class tittered and the teacher huffed, going back to the lesson.

"Don't be mean to people who control your grade point average," Luke muttered in my ear. "Especially since it's December of our senior year. We're almost free."

"Too late," I grumbled back.

"What?" Jess asked distractedly, still taking notes.

"Nothing," I said, and we grinned together as the bell rang.

"Praise the lord, it's lunchtime." Luke groaned as we walked down the hallway.

"You guys have lunch. I have AP bio," Jess said unhappily.

"Slackers unite," I said, high fiving Luke.

"I'll see you guys later." Jess laughed, walking away.

The two slackers that were left stopped by my locker. I exchanged the textbooks in my backpack for the ones I needed in the last two periods of the day. Luke leaned against the adjacent lockers and pretended not to notice his admirers while he ran his hand through his thick brown hair.

"Stop or you'll give them a heart attack," I teased, gesturing to his audience of underclassmen.

He winked at them and they all dispersed with reddened faces. I don't blame them. If I hadn't known Luke since freshmen year his green eyes would make me melt. "Jealous much," he taunted lightly.

"You wish," I said, rolling my eyes.

"You wish I wished," he retorted.

"You wish I wished you wished," I argued.

"No more," he said, throwing up his hands. "This is starting to sound like a really dumb Disney movie."

"Can't have that," I agreed, walking towards the lunchroom. Luke joined the lunch line to buy barely edible food (you'd think that as high as the tuition here was, they could afford something with higher class than taco Tuesday) while I went to sit down at a table with our other friends.

Our friends slowly filled the table as the cafeteria buzz heightened to a loud chatter, pieces of conversation brushing by us. Luke took his regular seat next to me, and our friends slowly followed. We left an empty seat in memory of poor Jess who had taken two sciences for extra credit and hadn't been affected by senioritis yet. It was always the one next to me, as a symbol of Jess's right hand man-ness to me. Of course, sometimes rugby playing assholes sat in it, like was currently happening.

"Hey Riley," Clayton Devis, a completely gorgeous blonde with as much substance as a school lunch and a stuck-up mindset—very stereotypically Conlet Academy, leered at me, leaning too close for my comfort. "Looks like I picked the right table to sit at today." Repulsed, I leaned all the way back into Luke.

"What do you want, Devis?" I asked, wrinkling my nose at him.

"What, I can't sit with my," he glanced around the group, "favorite," he made a choking sound, "people without being questioned?"

"Well, since you barely recognize us as people, let alone your favorites, I can't help but think that you're up to something," I replied, studying him carefully. Then it clicked. "So you *just* found out about the curse, right?" (More on that later. Right now, I'm trying to set up some context for you guys. You're welcome.)

"What curse?" He frowned, in almost believable innocence.

"Nice try," I said, shaking my head. "But I can't control who breaks that. Go back to your girlfriend." (He's dating Sterling, by the way. They complement each other's personalities perfectly.)

"Fine, but if you change your mind..." He stood up, tilting his head down into my personal space, "you know where to find me."

I pushed him away, sitting upright in my chair again. "Don't hold your breath." I thought about it for a second and held up one finger. "I take that back. Please hold your breath. I've heard that idiocy can be

8

transported through the air and I can feel my brain cells screaming for help." Luke gave me a subtle high five behind my back as I waved with my other hand to Clayton while he stormed back to his table.

"Nice one." Luke chuckled, still watching Clayton's face. I turned back to my lunch, picking at the yogurt that I had packed this morning. "You okay?" Luke murmured in my ear. I shrugged and nodded.

"I should be used to this by now, right?"

"I guess," Luke said, stretching his long arms behind his head.

"Does anyone really ever get used to hot boys coming up to you and trying to be your true love by your eighteenth birthday?" my friend Crystal said with a breathy sigh. "Damn your luck, Riley."

Luke leaned away from her to roll his eyes. Only he and Jess knew how I really felt about my curse. "You can have the whole 'fall asleep, be wrapped in thorns and then kissed by a random stranger who will then become my husband as soon as I am a legal adult and then the mayor of this town by association,'" I said, with a laugh that was badly forced. "I'll take all of the hot boys hitting on me until then."

"Sorry, it doesn't work that way. Those are mutually exclusive," she decided.

The rest of my day passed normally. School ended, I went to Luke's house (scratch that: mansion) and then I went to my house (mansion). And by the time my head hit the pillow it was already another day.

Chapter Three

uke doesn't like the way I'm telling the story. He doesn't think he has a big enough part, so he gets to narrate for a while. And if he says anything incredibly offensive about me just ignore it because I already promised I wouldn't read his part or edit it. Good luck; you're now entering the mind of a teenage boy. Beware.

Luke—now

I groaned when my alarm went off and rolled out of bed, literally, landing with a thump on the floor. "Luke it's time for school," I heard my mom yell from the floor below me.

"I'm up," I shouted back. That wasn't really a lie; I was awake, I just wasn't up*right*. I stood up, pulling on the first pair of khakis that I could find. Then a white undershirt and the light blue button up of the Conlet Academy uniform. I ran a comb through my hair and brushed my teeth before running downstairs.

"Your dad's driving you," my mom said as she pecked me on the cheek and handed me a waffle.

"Thanks," I mumbled, through a mouthful of Eggo.

"Have a good day," she called after me. I waved while closing the door leading to the garage behind me.

"Morning," my dad grumbled when I got into the car. He wasn't a morning person either.

"Gmph," I replied, half sleep and half waffle forming the word. I finished the waffle in the car and washed it down with the water my dad handed me. "Thanks," I said, when I finally came up for air.

"Gmph," he responded.

"Gmph," I agreed, leaning my head against the window. I stopped by the cafeteria to buy Riley a quick cup of coffee, before heading to her locker where I knew she'd be. She'd hung out at her locker every morning since freshmen year of high school. I could feel a smile creeping up my lips when I saw her, puffy eyed from lack of sleep. She was leaning against her locker, with Jess talking in her ear.

"Why are you always so happy in the morning," she grumbled when she saw me. Her face brightened when I handed her the coffee, her endless blue eyes catching the light and reflecting it a million times brighter. "You're a life saver," she beamed, her smile melting my soul and reforming it into a less manly shape, like a marshmallow. This is what it had come to. Marshmallows.

A pack of guys walked past, wolf whistling when they saw her. She flipped them off. Guys hitting on her made me want to hit them, but she never seemed fazed by it. She glanced up from her coffee and saw me staring at her. I wanted to look away, but she caught my eye and gave me her Mona Lisa smile. I grinned like, I assume, an idiot until a group of underclassmen girls walked past me, waving flirtatiously. Riley looked away, rolling her eyes at them; I cursed them under my breath.

The bell rang and Riley pushed herself off of her locker into a standing position. "See you later," she said, putting her leather messenger bag over her shoulder and hooking arms with Jess. They walked off in the opposite direction together, heads bent close as they giggled in each other's ears.

"Bye," I called. Riley smiled over her shoulder at me until the hoards of people obscured her completely.

"Hey man," someone called from behind me. I turned around and groaned. Clayton was pushing his way through the bevy of bodies going in all different directions.

"Great," I groaned to myself.

"So you and Riley? What's that about?" He laughed obnoxiously.

"Nothing's going on with me and Riley," I answered through gritted

11

teeth. Even his breath projected stupidity. I started to walk to class.

"So you don't mind if I take a shot then right 'cause damn," he whistled.

"What about your girlfriend?" Twenty feet to my classroom.

"I don't know," he replied. Ten more feet. "She just doesn't have that," he gesticulated a crude woman with curves, "that Riley has. Riley's smokin'." A few split knuckles were nothing compared to the look on his face that I got to enjoy after I had broken his nose.

The headmaster stood in front of us, arms crossed, with a look that could only be described as *I'm not mad, I'm just disappointed.* Clayton was holding the bloody tissue to his nose, slouching pitifully in his chair. "Do you boys want to tell me how this started so we can all get back to class?" Headmaster Jameson asked calmly, eyes searching us carefully.

"I was just walking behind him, and he turned around and hit me," Clayton said, holding up the hand that wasn't covered in blood.

"I don't believe that for a second, Mr. Devis," Jameson said evenly. "Luke?"

"What he said," I grumbled glancing at the clock. "Can I go to class now?"

"Clayton can go to class," Jameson said, waving his hand dismissively at him, "but you and I need to have a talk I think." Clayton smirked at me as he left, subtly holding up his middle finger behind his back. "I saw that," Jameson called after him. It was my turn to smirk at his reddening face as he disappeared out of sight. "What really happened?" Jameson asked after getting up to shut the door. He perched on the edge of his desk and eyed me wisely.

"What he said," I repeated.

"Luke, I've seen your record. And I've seen his. He gets punched a lot. I'm starting to think that it's not a coincidence."

"It's definitely not," I agreed.

"So what happened?"

I took a deep breath and sized him up. "You're not going to let me go until I tell you what really happened, are you?"

A small smile appeared and he nodded. "I knew all those As couldn't be an accident."

"He insulted my friend. I punched him. That's it," I said.

12

"Which friend?"

"Riley Owens."

"Ah," he said nodding, with a mischievous spark in his warm, brown eyes. "In that case, I think that two hours of Saturday detention for the next three Saturdays is punishment enough. You're dismissed."

"Thanks," I said, meaning it. Jameson was definitely one of the better adults at the school. I paused at the door, turning around. "What happens if Clayton's parents decide to press charges?"

"We tell them that you hit him by accident in the crowded hallway, and if he decides to argue then he can tell his old-fashioned dad that he was bullying a girl and got his comeuppance," he answered, looking at me from behind his desk.

"Thank you," I said again, smiling.

"Close the door behind you," was all he said. I closed it quietly and checked my phone. Twenty minutes before my next class started. It wasn't worth it; I was supposed to be in Spanish. I chose instead to wait outside of Riley's physics classroom, spending the extra time playing Tetris on my phone.

"Hey," she said, when the bell had rung and people began spilling into the already tight hallway.

"Hey," I replied, narrowly dodging a freshman, in a full sprint to his next class.

"What are you doing here?" Jess asked suspiciously. "Isn't your Spanish class like halfway across the school?" I rubbed the back of my head guiltily, spiking up and then smoothing down my floppy hair.

"What happened to your hands?" Riley gasped, cradling one of them in her own. They were embarrassingly sweaty and bloody, but I resisted the urge to cringe away and wipe them on a passing sophomore.

"You should see the other guy," I said with a laugh. That wasn't a lie; the other guy did look much worse than I did.

"Who's the other guy?" She frowned.

"No one," I said cheerfully, shivering slightly when she ran her fingers lightly over mine. But, of course with my luck, Clayton walked by just as I said that, casting a fearful glance at me. Riley followed my gaze and hit me lightly on the shoulder when she saw who it was.

"Did you do that?" she asked coolly.

13

"Maybe." I winced, twisting my fingers so I was holding her hand now. She pulled away and rolled her eyes at me.

"Do I want to know why?"

"Probably not."

"Fair enough." She shrugged, walking towards our history classroom.

"Will you at least tell me?" Jess asked when Riley was out of earshot. I shot her a secretive smile while walking backwards, before turning around and entering the class.

"What does that mean?" she hissed after me.

I took my usual seat in the back row, two seats behind where Riley usually sat. Today, she sat right in front of me. I shot her a questioning look while the teacher turned off the lights and pulled down the projector screen. She turned around, scribbling on a piece of paper. I looked past her to the disturbing pictures our teacher was showcasing until a neatly folded square landed in my lap. I unfolded it slowly, watching her grow more and more impatient. I grinned teasingly at her while pulling one corner slowly open. She narrowed her eyes at me until I opened it fully and looked down to read it. *Tell me!* was all it said. I shook my head cheerfully, knowing exactly what she meant. She grimaced at me and turned back around to listen to the lesson.

The period flew by; I didn't take in a single fact about the French revolution but that test would be failed for a good cause. Of course, if there were a test for creepy people who all but stalked their best friends then I would pass that one with flying colors. I would have a 4.0 GPA if there were an extra credit class on the little things that Riley did. Like how she tilted her head when she took notes, and she held the paper at a diagonal so she wouldn't have to write straight across. And how her lines sloped slightly downward at the ends of the sentences. Her hair kept spilling onto my desk, and I had to sit on my hands to keep them from playing with the perfectly waved silk. Okay next topic, this is getting a little creepy. It is a bonus that you guys know way more about Riley now than I'm assuming you wanted to.

English was English and lunch was lunch and by the end of the day I could barely form full sentences. I wonder if boredom mixed with lack of sleep kills as many brain cells as getting punched in the face does, 'cause then Clayton and I were even. "My house or yours?" I asked Riley when we met at her locker after the final bell. She looked at me weirdly. "What?"

"It's Wednesday."

"I know that."

"We always go to Jess's house on Wednesday," she said, putting a cool hand on my forehead. "Are you feeling okay?"

"I just thought you might want to change things up," I grumbled, sticking out my tongue at her. "No need to be mean."

"There's always a need to be mean," she said and grinned, shoving more books than should fit in her bag and slinging it over her shoulder.

"Ready to go?" Jess asked, coming up behind us.

"Will you please tell Luke that he's crazy," Riley ridiculed me. "He asked me whose house I wanted to go to today."

"Are you okay?" Jess frowned concernedly, without the sarcasm that Riley had infused into her sentence.

"I'm fine," I said and laughed. "I just wanted to know if we were going to switch it up. Never mind, I regret asking."

"Good, you should," Riley said, satisfied. We walked to Jess's house in silence; well I was silent. Riley and Jess never shut up when they were together. I had learned to tune out the giggling.

"Peanut butter?" Jess asked rhetorically, pointing at Riley when we had made it to her house and were raiding her kitchen. "And Goldfish."

"Please," Riley and I agreed. Jess handed Riley a container of Skippy peanut butter and a spoon, and me, a bag of Goldfish.

"Thanks," I said, already stuffing the crackers in my mouth. She grabbed an apple for herself and we sat down in their kitchen, with the vaulted ceilings included of course. A Racheston classic. "So what are studying today?" I asked through a mouthful of Goldfish.

"The original?" Jess suggested.

"No more reading." Riley groaned, putting her head down on her folded arms. "Let's watch the *Disney* version of *Sleeping Beauty*."

"Yes, please," Jess agreed tiredly.

"I hate to be the voice of reason, but your birthday's Christmas Eve. That's about a month which means we should do real research." I said with a heavy sigh.

"What's the use?" Riley grumbled. "I'm doomed to be useless under a curse and then be married to whoever wakes me up."

"To be fair," Jess started. Riley glared darkly at her but Jess pushed on. "You'll know who it is. He's going to come to town before the curse because his parents briefed him."

"So?" Riley said. "Are you saying that this is okay because I'm going to meet the person that I'm doomed to marry?"

"You guys can go on a couple dates! It's not like he's a complete stranger that's going to kiss you," Jess said.

"Well that makes it better," Riley decided, with a heavy enough dose of sarcasm to practically make my ears ring. I'm surprised Jess didn't melt from the full impact.

"Can we at least figure out who's going to cast the spell on you?" I asked, deciding to intervene before Jess actually did shatter under Riley's frigid gaze.

"No," she replied, looking away from Jess long enough to eat another spoonful of peanut butter. "This curse has been in my family for too long. And I can't exactly ask my mom. She's already designing how she's going to redo my room while I'm asleep for a hundred years, or until a prince comes along."

"We can try and make the prince that's coming fall in love with you in a month," Jess proposed.

"No," I said firmly.

Riley gave me a weird look, and turned to Jess. "I'd rather figure out how to save myself."

"You say that every day. We've been researching for three years and we haven't figured anything out yet. Doesn't that say something?" Jess snapped. Riley and I exchanged worried looks. Jess never spoke higher than her usual sweet voice. "Sorry," she said, looking ashamed. "I'm just worried about you. You know that, right?"

"Of course I know that," Riley smiled, laying her hand on top of Jess's. "It'll be okay."

Three years ago

Riley (because Luke doesn't know everything about my life and would be terrible at telling this story)

I paused at my mailbox, before trekking up the long, sloping driveway—more of a private road than a driveway I guess—stopping short when I finally reached the end and the road opened into a green lawn, and a semi-circle of pavement, usually empty but now littered with expensive looking cars. I swore under my breath. I forgot that it was Friday; Friday was tea and biscuit day for the other rich housewives, and apparently, it was my mom's turn to host.

I chewed my lip indecisively. I had to get to my room to do homework, and I would be safe in there. But then I ran the risk of having to make polite small talk; having only started high school two weeks ago, any conversation I was forced into would probably center on how many friends I had made. And so far, I had only made two. I could see my window from here, glittering welcomingly in the warm September sun. I stuffed the mail into my backpack, and walked carefully over to the lawn. I skirted the edges of the "forest" (it was just a smattering of trees, faultlessly groomed) until I finally reached the corner of the front part of my house. I crawled under the big bay windows that looked out into the front yard, standing up and dusting myself off when I was safely at the decorative shutters. I examined the tree that grew about a foot to the left of my room. The branches by my window were thin and fragile, but the rest of it seemed climbable. I clipped my backpack around my waist—it was light; thank god for the freshmen year workload—and tested the first branch with my foot. It was a good thing I hadn't reached my combat boot phase yet, or I wouldn't have survived. The white tennis shoes I had been wearing were permanently stained from my army crawl through grass, however. A worthy sacrifice at the time. It held, and I grabbed the next branch to pull myself up.

"Riley!" my mom cried from below me, when I had made it about halfway to my window. "What do you think you're doing?"

"Climbing a tree," I answered cheerfully. "What do you think I'm doing?"

She glowered at me and pointed forcefully at the ground. "Get down

17

here now," she said, teeth gritted in a polite smile. She glanced fearfully at the windows that were, thankfully, empty.

I sighed, resigned to my fate of falsely happy housewives. I descended carefully, jumping down to the ground when I was close enough. I unclipped my backpack and handed her the mail. "Nice talking to you," I said, brushing past her into the house. I kicked off my shoes at the door and assessed my chances. The kitchen was next to the curving staircase, but maybe finger sandwiches were interesting enough to keep them from actual human contact.

I crept to the stairs, safe until "Girls, come say hi to Riley," was ordered from behind me. The jovial chattering paused, as one by one the happy housewives came out of the kitchen.

"Riley," they all cried together like a rich person cult. They all waltzed up to me, pecking my cheek with hard impersonal kisses. Did they understand that this was Massachusetts not Los Angeles?

"Nice to see you," I said politely, just like I had been taught to.

My mom nodded, satisfied. "Why don't you come sit with us in the kitchen?"

"Actually, I have a lot of homework," I lied. The lazy ladies looked scandalized.

"Who assigns homework on a Friday?" Damn I was caught.

"My math teacher wants us to practice over the weekend," I said, the courteous smile starting to hurt my face.

"Well you have all weekend," my mom said sweetly. "Come spend time with us!" She linked arms with me and half dragged me to the kitchen. They poured me a cup of tea. I added as much sugar as I could while they weren't watching and zoned out, their dull chatter making my head throb. My eyes settled on the window, absorbed in my own thoughts, until I was snapped out of it by a swift kick to my shin. I sat up straighter, almost spilling my tea.

"What?"

"Ms. Sherton wants to know how you like high school," my mom repeated, her fingertips turning white from pressing into her teacup. Told you.

"It's much better than middle school." I smiled in the general direction of who I thought might be Ms. Sherton. My mom gestured faintly to the woman across from me with fluffed blonde hair. I really needed to learn their names. All the women nodded, pleased, and went back to their talk about the upcoming benefits. I went back to looking out the window, until I heard my name.

"You were right dear," Ms. Sherton was saying to my mom, unashamedly studying me, from shoes to face. "You should have no problem with her, really. Any young boy would be happy to kiss her I'm sure."

"Why would I have to be kissed?" I laughed, thinking that this conversation proved this cult's ideals once and for all. My mom shook her head, her eyes pleading with me. "What?"

"To wake you up." Ms. Sherton frowned, eyebrows crinkling together into a blonde caterpillar. "Surely your mom has discussed your duties?"

"Duties," I choked, imagining this woman having the birds and the bees talk with me in front of everyone.

"On your eighteenth birthday," a different woman added. They were all staring at me. Then they shifted their attention to my mother.

"Oh dear." Ms. Sherton clucked her tongue.

My mom shifted uncomfortably, pulling her pencil skirt farther down on her legs. "We were going to give her another couple of years before we told her. She's only fourteen." The women nodded and dropped the subject in favor of another mind-numbing topic (you'd think they'd have to talk about something interesting eventually. For goodness sake, there aren't that many girly topics in the world).

"What about my eighteenth birthday," I interrupted them, but no one paid attention. I left my teacup on the table and ran all the way to Luke's house. I had to ring the buzzer at the gate. I wasn't sure he'd let me in since we'd only met two weeks ago, but the gates swung open anyway. "Do you know anything about my eighteenth birthday?" I panted as soon as he opened the door.

"That you'll be turning eighteen?" he answered questioningly. "Is it a trick question?"

"Never mind," I said, turning around to leave as soon as I realized how gross I probably was from running four blocks.

"No, come in," he said, laughing. "You look like you need water.

19

And maybe chocolate? Do girls like that?" I grinned and nodded, accepting the invitation. Twenty minutes later I was sitting on his living room floor with a cookie and a bottle of sparkling water. (We can't have regular water in Racheston or it goes against the rich person code). I told him what I knew, and he listened carefully. "I don't know what to tell you," he shrugged when I had finished, "but we can figure it out."

"Really?" I asked, surprised.

"Sure," he said, walking away and coming back with a laptop. "How hard can it be to find answers? Google has everything, right?" He sat next to me and we spent the next hour coming up with increasingly ridiculous keywords to search. I feel like Google started to judge us after we asked it *how many rich women does it take to eat a finger sandwich.* Don't even ask how we got there. We didn't learn anything, but by dinnertime I felt better about my situation.

"I can go home now," I said, catching my breath after laughing over Google's answer to our question.

"Are you kidding?" he asked, still chuckling, checking the time. "Just stay for dinner!"

"I don't want to intrude." I winced, thinking about how mad my mom would be if she found out I had invited myself to eat with a family I didn't know.

"It's not intruding if I tell you to stay," he said and winked with those amazing green eyes. So I said yes and that was the beginning of a beautiful friendship. I still go to dinner at his house every Friday because I like his family a lot more than I like mine.

Okay I'm letting Luke narrate again. I hope you guys miss me. If he's annoying you, just skip to chapter four. Then it's my turn to talk.

Luke—Now

I reread *Briar Rose* for the millionth time, groaning when I reached the same ending that was always there. They lived happily ever after; weird for the Grimm brothers. Maybe they decided that any girl who was already forced to sleep for a hundred years and then had to be kissed by a random stranger deserved a happy ending. Or maybe they just felt bad for the poor prince who had to kiss a random dusty girl. "I hate to tell you this," I said to Riley, who was skimming a spell book, "but your only chances of not sleeping for a hundred years are to find a true love or a magical fairy."

She looked up, frustrated, and glared at me. "I don't want a true love. I don't want to get married at eighteen. I don't want to be a submissive housewife and I don't want to get kissed by some random guy!"

"Fairy?" I suggested again, holding the storybook up as a shield in case she decided to punch me.

She moaned and flopped down onto her arms. "Where the hell am I going to find a fairy in Massachusetts?" I rubbed her shoulder in comfort; we'd had this conversation every Wednesday when we came over to Jess's to do research.

"Have you talked to your parents about it?" I said out of habit, almost like I was reading off of a script.

"My mom went through this too, you know," she said, propping her hand on her cheek to frown at me. "She loves it. All of it. When she was my age and found out about our curse the only preparation effort she made was to moisturize more so that her skin wouldn't dry up when she was asleep. And then my dad woke her up and they got married and they're still so happy that she wants that for me, and my dad's too scared to fight against her because he thinks that this curse is the way to avoid paying for college, and besides he'll never have to worry about the prince breaking my heart because we're supposed to be bonded together for all of eternity when he wakes me up," she said, finishing her sentence in one rushed breath and collapsing back onto the table.

"Why don't you go with it?" Jess asked, also holding up a book in defense. "I think it's romantic that a guy would cut through thorns to kiss you," she added dreamily. Riley didn't even look up. She just grumbled mutedly from where she was.

"How do you know there'll be thorns?" I queried over Riley's head to Jess.

"Have you seen a version without thorns? Because the only ones I've seen had thorns."

21

"The only one you've seen is the Disney version," I said, rolling my eyes.

"The original has thorns too," Jess argued.

"Touché," Riley said, barely making sound with her head buried in her arms.

"Shut up, you're not in this," I joked.

"True," she agreed, sitting up. "It's not like it's my life or anything."

"Exactly," I said, nodding sagely.

She laughed sadly and flopped back down to the table. "Sure feels that way," came the muffled response. I reached over and smoothed her hair comforting and she flicked my hand without sitting up.

"Fine, be mean," I teased, withdrawing my arm.

"Thanks, I will be," she retorted, looking at me from under her arms. Her mascara was blurred into streams from her eyes.

"You got a little," I trailed off, gesturing to my face. She started to wipe it off self-consciously but gave up and smeared it into greater effect.

"Better?" she asked, sticking her tongue out.

"Much," I nodded. Then I read *Briar Rose* for the million and first time.

Riley and I walked home around five; we always walked together because she lived about four blocks away from me, which in Racheston terms was about two and a half mansions. "You coming in?" I asked when we neared my house. She checked her phone and bit her lip in indecision.

"It's five fifteen already," she said, "but I also don't want to go home."

"Is your mom going to care?"

"Probably." She said, glancing longingly at my front gates and glancing down at her grumbling stomach. "But your mom's an amazing cook and I don't want to wait until Friday for her to make me comfort food. My mom's probably making some low-calorie dinner with lettuce and kale."

"Why?" I asked, shaking my head. "Weren't you all cursed with forever perfect bodies or whatever?"

"I wish." She laughed. "I think it's just good genetics," she added, smoothing her plaid uniform over her long legs.

"Same," I said, pretending to pull down a skirt of my own. She grinned and punched me lightly on the arm. "Come on," I said, grabbing her wrist and dragging her towards my house. "My mom can call yours and explain. You know your mom loves mine."

"True," she hesitated.

"Come on!"

"Fine," she finally consented, giving in and letting me drag her through my front door. We kicked off our shoes, just in time for my old golden retriever to come running and jump on her, which was saying something since he hardly ever ran for anything. "Hi." She laughed as he licked her face.

"I can't tell if your gift with animals is a magical Disney princess thing or if you wear, like, gravy perfume," I said, watching her try not to get knocked down with amusement.

"It's that gravy perfume," she said, finally managing to get his paws off her shoulder, leaving muddy footprints on her bleached white shirt, "never leave home without it."

"Sorry." I laughed, reining him back. He lunged forward again, dragging me with him.

"It's fine," she said, grinning and wiping slobber off her face.

"But he did fix your mascara problem," I said brightly, motioning to my eyes.

"Shut up," she said, making an obscene gesture in Italian with her chin and her hand.

"Damn, Owens," I said, shaking my head in disapproval. "Go do that again in front of the security cameras."

"Pass!" she said, smiling sweetly. I opened my mouth to retort but my mom saved her at the nick of time.

"Riley," my mom cried, sounding pleasantly surprised. "What are you doing here, dear? We weren't expecting you until Friday."

"Hi, Mrs. Moore," she replied cheerfully, "I was hoping you'd have some mashed potatoes for me today."

"Of course, sweetie," my mom said, making an attempt to brush the mud off Riley's shoulders, and wincing when it didn't come off. "I'm sorry about this, I forgot he was outside and by the time I thought to let

23

him in he had dug up half the yard," she added, throwing up her hands in despair.

"It's okay," Riley said, grinning over her shoulder at me as my mom led her into our warm kitchen. "I have another shirt for tomorrow."

"I'm sure Lucas wouldn't mind lending you a shirt until you get home," my mom volunteered, giving me 'the look'.

"Of course, come on," I said to Riley.

"Be right back," she told my mom.

"How much mashed potatoes do you want? I'll reheat some while you're upstairs," mom called after us.

"Just a bowl, please," Riley shouted back. "I love your mom," she said to me.

"It's mutual," I assured her. "She never stops talking about you."

"Sounds about right," she teased, flipping a sheet of hair over her shoulder.

"Here," I said, tossing her a t-shirt.

"Are you going to leave so I can change?"

"You're not bothering me," I said, sitting down on my bed. She picked up a pair of pants from my floor and threw them at my face. "Fine, fine, I'm going, just no more violence. Please. For the children."

"Fine," she agreed, "but only for the children. Not for you." She struck a dramatic pose.

"It's too bad we don't have children then," I said, escaping before she could throw any more articles of clothing at me. My mom handed me a bowl of reheated potatoes when I got into the kitchen, and I sat down to savor them while waiting for Riley. She came down about five minutes later, tugging on the shirt. It went down to the middle of her thighs and was way too loose around her arms and stomach. "Quite the look," I said chuckling, barely resisting the urge to tell her that she looked just as beautiful as usual.

"You should know," she responded, picking at the shirt with her fingers. "You actually wear this."

"Not since middle school," I said, defending my never changing clothes.

"Sure," she grinned, "that explains why it was at the front of your drawer."

"Fine," I grumbled. "You're too perceptive for me, Riley Owens." She bowed mockingly and sat down next to me.

My mom handed her another bowl of potatoes; she took a steaming bite, and recoiled. "Oh hot." She winced. Then she took another bite anyway.

"Idiot," I said fondly.

"It's not my fault that it's delicious. Thanks, Mrs. Moore."

"No problem," mom said, sitting at the table with us. "So, Lucas, anything interesting happen today?" She gave me a piercing look with her warm green eyes.

"Not unless you've heard something," I muttered into my potatoes.

"Interesting look for your knuckles," she remarked, glaring at me, "considering that you left the house today intact."

"Can we talk about this later?" I asked, looking at Riley, who was uncomfortably staring at her potatoes.

"Of course." My mom sighed, a contrite smile appearing. "Sorry Riley dear, I'm sure you didn't come here to talk about how Lucas is grounded."

"What?" I protested. She silenced me with a look.

"Please don't ground him, Mrs. Moore," Riley begged. "We need him, especially with my eighteenth birthday approaching." She choked on the words.

My mom sized me up, finally relenting. "Fine. But home at eleven from whichever house you're at. And nothing this weekend. You kids can come here to research."

"Deal," Riley smiled.

"Are we all forgetting whose life this is?" I asked grouchily.

"Are we forgetting which one of your friends just saved your social life?" my mom countered. I ate my potatoes in silence after that, while Riley and my mom prattled on like old friends.

Finally, Riley checked the clock and jumped out of her seat. "I have to go, I'm sorry. I forgot to tell my mom I was staying at your house," she said, tugging unsurely at the shirt she was wearing.

"Keep it," I said. "It's not like I don't know where you live."

"Thanks," she said, smiling gratefully. She gave my mom a quick hug and all but ran out the door, after giving my dog a quick ear rub of course.

"Such a nice girl," my mom said, cleaning up the dishes, and the conversation was over.

Chapter Four

oor Luke. I bet you all skipped to chapter four because you missed me so much, right?

My day started with a random hot guy in my kitchen (not a bad way to start a Thursday, I have to say). I went through my normal routine; I brushed my hair and then my teeth, got dressed and put on the minimum amount of makeup that was still socially acceptable. I grabbed my backpack from where I had left it the night before, and walked slowly down the stairs, absorbed in trying to remember if it was a chemistry test that I had today or a global essay. "Hi," I said to my mom.

"Good morning," she said and smiled, handing me an apple in place of the banana that I was reaching for (it's better for the skin of someone who's going to sleep for a long time, she says).

"Hi," I said to my dad, who nodded with a grunt. I could tell that the coffee hadn't kicked in yet. "Hi," I said to the random blonde boy sitting at my table. I had walked about halfway down my hall before I had to retrace my steps and poke my head back into the kitchen. "Do I want to know who he is?"

"This is Prince Alexander of," she paused, fluttering a hand as if

27

trying to remember something, then shaking it off. "Prince Alexander," she said lovingly, handing him scrambled eggs.

"And who is…" I started, distracting by the food. "Wait, why does he get eggs?"

"Heroes need their strength," my mom replied, rubbing his head affectionately.

It finally sank in why a prince was sitting at my table in a small Massachusetts town, four weeks before I was supposed to be woken up from a deep cursed sleep. I agreed with my legs, which wanted to run. "Gross," I shuddered, glaring at all of them. "I still have a month, you know."

"His parents wanted him to come early so that you would have a chance to get to know each other before he has to save you." My mom shrugged, smoothing down her sweater like she could tell I was about to have a temper tantrum.

"Hey," the boy said, in a disgustingly attractive voice, standing up and holding out his hand. "I'm Alex, I'm here to be your true love and…"

"I know," I said cutting him off, ignoring his sultry smile and turning on my heel. "Bye," I called running back down the hall.

"Riley," my mom yelled at me, her voice shrilly polite, "come back and say hello to Alex, please."

"No thanks," I shouted back. "I'm going to be late to school."

"Riley!" Her cry echoed after I had closed the door. I shuddered to myself and took my time walking to school. Even after walking two steps a minute, I was twenty minutes early. I dragged my feet all the way to my locker and sluggishly exchanged my textbooks, closing my locker and sliding down to the ground. I brought my knees to my chest and wrapped my arms around them, burying my head and taking deeply aching breaths. This was all getting too real. I still had another month of freedom. I measured my breathing carefully, keeping the tears out of my eyes. Then I remembered that I was wearing a skirt and put my legs down even though I was all alone in the hallway. I settled for crossing my arms tightly across my stomach, constricting it and making my heart slow down.

"You look like you're about to throw up," Luke's voice floated down from above me. I didn't even look up; I was too busy having my first actual panic attack, not counting the ones I had had about school and boys and school and school. "Are you okay?" he asked, starting to get concerned. He sat down next to me and tilted my head with his hand so that I had to look at him. "What's wrong?"

"He came," I shivered, still shaking. He wrapped his arms around me, drawing me into his chest.

"I'm going to skip the inappropriate joke and just ask who." That made me smile. "See, I knew you still had a sense of humor. Who came?"

"You know." I motioned with my hands in the general sense of a crown. "The guy who has to…" I trailed off.

"Ah," Luke nodded, loosening his grip, but tightening it again when I squirmed closer. "It's fine, we'll just go to Jess's house again instead of yours today."

"That's fine for you people, but some of us actually sleep in that house every day." I groaned, imagining the mornings for the next month. My mom would probably give 6:00 a.m. tours through my bedroom to show him what I looked like when I was sleeping so he wouldn't be surprised when the time actually came.

"Can you stay at Jess's?"

"For the next month?"

"True, that's a long time. Just go back when you know your mom has the happy housewives meeting and pick up clothes then leave again. You can stay with me, you know my mom loves you," he offered.

"That wouldn't look scandalous at all." I laughed, even with the dull twinge in my side telling me to accept.

"People already think we're dating," he said shrugging. "This would just cement the idea in their heads."

"No cementing anything please," I said, massaging my temples. "And no one thinks we're dating, believe me. Every girl in our class would be after me if they did."

"Can I help it if I'm incredibly handsome?" he asked, posing. "No, so don't blame me." I grinned and pinched his cheeks like an old auntie.

"It's the dimples," I told him, standing up and brushing myself off as other people began to fill the hallway.

29

"So true," he agreed, green eyes twinkling devilishly.

"You're here early," Jess remarked as she walked up to us.

"Unfortunately." I sighed, running my hand through my hair and collecting it into a ponytail.

"What?" Jess said, looking behind me. I turned around to see Luke making the universal sign for 'stop' by pretending to cut his neck. When he saw me looking he held his hands behind his back.

"Nothing," he said innocently.

"Right," I laughed, picking up my bag from the ground. "Come on. Let's go to class."

The day went by quickly. I was zoned out in all of my classes, thoughts miles away; this caused all of my teachers to call on me for not listening, regrettably. I checked my phone as more and more texts from my mom popped up in the messages. *Come home now,* one read. Like that was going to happen. *Rude this morning to Alex. Apologize now.* Unless he came to all of my classes and I had to get a restraining order there was no way that I was talking to him until we were married with four kids and I absolutely had to. But only to tell him that I wanted a divorce of course. *No* was all I sent back.

"Miss Owens, is that a phone?" my chemistry teacher snapped, in the middle of her lesson on light.

"It is," I replied, holding it out to her. "Please take it." The class laughed, thinking that I was mocking her; I really just needed an excuse not to talk to my mom anymore.

"You can get this from your dean at the end of the week," she snapped, pocketing it. Damn. The end of the week was tomorrow; that was too soon.

"That was rough," Luke said sympathetically while we were coming out of class.

"Are you kidding?" I laughed. "Now I have an excuse not to talk to my mom and her crazy ass. She keeps texting me that I need to come home and apologize for being rude to Alex."

"Alex," Luke said, wrinkling his nose. "Is that?"

"Yep," I said, shuddering.

"Poor Alex." Luke sighed sadly. "All he wanted to do was to kiss a nice sleeping girl and get married, but instead he's going to fight through

30

thorns for nothing."

"Well from what it looks like, he's still going to get to kiss a sleeping girl and get married, but I'm sure as hell not going to be nice about it."

"Just bite the guy for me when you wake up," Luke said, looking downright mischievous.

"I would, but he seems like he'd be one of those boys who would be into that," I said with a wink.

"Was that necessary?"

"Completely."

"Well you can always practice on me if you want," he offered, leaning down to my level.

"Thanks." I laughed, pushing him away, keenly aware of everyone in the hallway watching us. "When I want to turn half of the school, the girl half, against me, I'll give you a call."

"You can just call Alex," he said, with a weird expression on his face. "Isn't he supposed to be prince charming? So perfect in every way possible?"

"Aw," I said, reaching up and patting his head. "Is someone worried that he's not the prettiest boy in Racheston anymore? It's ok you'll always be my go-to guy for comfort food. Alex can't take that away from you."

"I feel so much better now," he said, with an exaggerated smile.

"At least you don't have to kiss the guy," I grumbled. "I can't imagine that anyone's breath can be good after a week, or however long it takes him to get through the thorns, of hibernating."

"Well, it's not like he has to kiss with tongue," he pointed out. "Wait," he turned around, "does he?"

"No, actually, I think frenching with a sleeping girl is too creepy even by Racheston standards."

"And not much is creepy by Racheston standards," he said wisely.

After school, we met by the lockers again to decide what we were going to do. "We can't go to my house," Jess said unhappily. "My parents are actually going to be home and they don't know I'm helping you with this curse stuff."

"Why would they care?" Luke asked frowning. "Shouldn't they be happy that you're helping someone?"

"You'd think, right? But they don't want me getting involved. They think if I get involved that I'd end up sleeping in a room full of thorns and bugs somewhere." Surprisingly dark coming from someone whose philosophy was "every day is a new day for new hugs".

"Don't say that," I begged, shuddering as I imagined it. "I hadn't even thought about the bugs yet."

"Don't worry," Luke said, patting me on the shoulder. "We'll make sure to cover you in bug spray before you go in."

"Especially my lips," I said. "Maybe we can poison Alex while he's waking me up and that will solve all my problems at once."

Chapter Five

ho's Alex?" Jess asked. Luke started in a not-so-subtle rendition of "Someday My Prince Will Come" from *Snow White*. "You're kidding," she gasped, grabbing my shoulders and shaking me. "How could you not tell me?"

"I forgot!" I cried, pulling away before she caused brain damage.

"How could you forget? I'm your best friend!"

"Actually," Luke cut in, "I think I'm her best friend. She told me first this morning." They both turned on me and I shielded my eyes, pretending not to see them.

"Don't worry, I love you both equally," I assured them.

"Obviously not," Jess said, dramatically throwing her arm across her forehead like she was an old southern belle about to faint. "I can tell when I'm not wanted."

"Stop." I giggled, grabbing her arm and forcing her into a hug (maybe I was going to be the pedophile). She remained stiff until I started to pull away, then she hugged me back.

"Fine, I guess a pity hug from you is more than I usually get," she said.

"Wait, I want a pity hug," Luke cried, wrapping his arms around both of us.

"Can't breathe," Jess gasped. Being the shortest, she was wedged in an unflattering position, somewhere in between Luke's armpit and my neck. We dissolved into laughter, catching weird looks from the surrounding people.

"Come on, we can go to the library," Luke suggested when he had caught his breath.

"Are you sure? They have things like *books* and *knowledge* there," I said, with a mocking shudder.

"Riley," he said, staring deeply into my eyes; I could feel the heat creeping up my cheeks. "I would brave books for you. That's how you know that friendship is real. Would Alex brave the grouchy public librarians for you?"

"I don't think Alex is looking for 'real friendship', so no I doubt it," I said cheerfully.

"Thanks for the image that I didn't need," he grumbled, pretending to throw up.

"Not in here please, Mr. Moore. Take it outside," Mr. Jameson said, laughing as he waved a hand across his nose, fanning the imaginary smell away.

"God, I love him," Luke said grinning after he had disappeared from sight.

"I knew it," Jess teased.

"Why are all the hot ones gay?" I whined, adopting a stereotypical white girl voice, which wasn't hard; the entirety of my school was stereotypical white people.

"Nice, guys," Luke said grumpily. "Thanks for that."

"No problem," Jess and I said in sync, walking out of the school and down the street that led to the public library. Luke trailed behind us muttering about the gay friend-zone and kicking rocks at the back of our heels.

"Classy," I called back to him through gritted teeth when one actually clipped my leg.

"At least my *aim's* straight," he retorted, but when I turned around to see if he was actually mad he winked at me. I rolled my eyes at him, and he kicked a rock directly into my calf. "Score," he congratulated himself, giving himself a high five. I held the door when we got to the library, just long enough for him to catch up to us and I then I let go. "I hope Alex knows how good his future wife is at revenge," he whispered in my ear, rubbing his arm.

"I feel like someone should probably warn him," I murmured back. We took a table in the back on the second floor where no one ever went, and explored the library looking for books. Luke and I found one together in Latin on black magic and painstakingly translated it with an app on his phone. Jess found a book for children's fairytales and read it cover-to-cover twice before she finally gave up. We left to get food around seven and came back, re-reading what we had found until the librarians announced over the loudspeaker that the library was now closed, and any additional people should make their way to the exits.

"Don't have to go home but you can't stay here," Luke said quietly, Jess catching my eye pityingly.

"I'll come stay with you if you want," Jess offered. "I'm sure your mom won't force Alex onto you if I'm there."

"Can you?" I begged, sure that I looked crazy and desperate.

"Of course," she replied, taking my hand. Luke took my other hand and they walked me home together.

Luke and I waited at the beginning of the driveway together while Jess ran home to get clothes for tomorrow. She came back panting and sweating, making us wait another ten minutes before we could go inside. I gave up trying to huddle for warmth and settled for hopping up and down as I started to lose feeling in my toes and the cold seeped through my jacket and the exposed part of skin on my legs started to turn blue. By the end of it, I was so desperate for a heating system that *I* was the one that had to drag *them* inside. Jess threw out her arm to stop me before I could enter the house. She finger combed my hair and then her own, straightening our uniforms in a frenzy before letting me pass. I gave her a startled look and she shrugged. "You might not like him but he's still hot. And some kind of royalty if you're going to be woken up by him."

"I didn't say that I didn't like him," I protested. "I just said that I didn't want to be married to him. I don't even know him. He might be nice, you never know." (By the way, I regretted those words a month later. Just saying.)

"See, that's the right attitude," Jess said, nodding contentedly.

"That's a terrible attitude," Luke grumbled to me, low enough that Jess couldn't hear. "What if you give him a chance and he ends up being a serial killer?" I laughed loudly, surprised. Jess turned around and glared at us suspiciously. "Nothing," Luke said, innocently glancing over his shoulder at me. I grinned conspiratorially at him and he winked. Jess opened my front door, kicking her shoes off to the side, like she had done a hundred times. Luke and I followed her example. I loved that Jess was more at home here than I was; showed the amazing parenting that my mom put in to people who shared her romantic view of life. I could hear the susurration of voices in the kitchen, and I motioned for Luke and Jess to be quiet. Maybe we could avoid this confrontation altogether.

"Riley, is that you?" my mom called down the hallway, and I sighed an interesting word (I feel like if my life was actually made into a sitcom I wouldn't have any lines because they'd have to bleep me out. My mom found it endlessly frustrating).

"Nice," Luke smirked, unfortunately having heard me.

"Thanks," I replied, grimacing in the direction of the kitchen. "It's me," I answered my mom, raising my voice.

"Come here," she said brightly, coming into the hallway. Her face darkened by the faintest, barely noticeable fraction. "What are they doing here?" she asked sweetly, a dark after-note to her words.

"Jess wants to stay the night, and Luke's here for moral support," I answered, matching her brilliantly polite smile, watt by watt.

"Moral support for what?"

"You know what," I said in a coldly practiced voice, a chill injected into the words before I could stop it. I brushed past her, taking Luke's hand and dragging him with me. Jess had already walked to the kitchen while I was talking to my mom, and I could hear her light giggle as she introduced herself.

"Maybe Jess will seduce him and he won't want to marry you," Luke suggested in my ear. I instinctively cringed closer to him when his lips brushed my ear and, mentally checking myself as my cheeks heated up.

"Maybe," I laughed quietly, voice breathy. I blushed even deeper when I heard it. We finished the dreaded march to the kitchen; my stomach fluttered unhelpfully when Luke adjusted his grip on my thankfully dry hand, and held on tighter. Alex shot out of his chair when I entered, then hesitated when he saw how I was practically clinging for dear life to Luke.

"Hi." He smiled shyly, holding out his hand, which I took with my right, preparing to shake it. Instead, he pulled me closer with it, and brushed his lips over the first three knuckles. Luke tensed next to me and I shot him a confused look.

"Hey," I smiled tightly. Maybe if I looked deranged enough he wouldn't want to wake me up and I could just hibernate peacefully for a hundred years until everyone I knew and loved was dead. Luke let go of my hand long enough to shake Alex's hand (he looked thankful that Alex hadn't kissed his too) before taking mine back and threading his fingers in the gaps between my own. It felt weirdly intimate, which of course set my face ablaze again, causing my mom to glare at Luke from across the kitchen. Oh, the domino effect branching out from one stupid appendage. Luke and Alex appeared to be having a staring contest, neither of them breaking eye contact when I cleared my throat. "Is dad home?" I asked my mom, in the hopes of stopping the ridiculous dick-measuring contest happening before us.

"No, he had to stay late," she said, noticing what the boys were doing for the first time. "Luke," she said, forcing him to look away in fear of being branded rude by her.

"Yes," he answered, smiling with more genuineness than she deserved from the subtle glare she was giving him.

"When do your parents want you home?"

"My curfew is eleven on school nights," he replied, faultlessly well mannered. Her smile tightened around the edges; rules of a good host restricting her ability to kick him out. I saw her gaze flick to the clock before coming to rest on me. I glanced at the clock too; there was an hour before Luke had to go and my mom would be able to shamelessly force me to interact with Alex. From the looks of it, Jess wouldn't be much of a barrier between my mom and me when it came to my 'prince'. An awkward silence descended onto us; Jess twirled her hair nervously while Luke squeezed my hand encouragingly and Alex tried to have silent communication when we made eye contact, which I blatantly ignored. "Did we ever do our English homework?" Luke asked uncomfortably, trying desperately to break it.

"I don't think we did," I said gratefully. Jess caught on after a few seconds and shook her head enthusiastically.

"We definitely didn't," she said, smiling apologetically at Alex.

"We should do that," I said, already backing out of the kitchen.

"If we don't want zeros on our grades, then probably," Luke agreed. We grabbed our backpacks from the door and ran up the stairs to my room, closing the door behind us. I flopped down on my bed, Luke choosing a seat in the beanbag chair across from me and Jess sitting down on the floor.

"We don't actually have to go back down," I said to Jess after a while. "We don't even technically have to leave this room." I smiled mischievously.

"That's never a good look," Luke said, watching me warily. I threw the door to my walk-in closet open with a flourish, pushing past the junk on my floor to the back wall and motioning for them to follow. I slid my hands down the wall until I found the catch, and opened the door cut into the drywall.

"Wow," Jess commented, looking surprised. "How did I not know about that?"

"My parents only built it like a year ago," I answered, squeezing through it. The ceiling sloped dramatically until I had to drop into a crawling position. I could hear them do the same behind me. It was only about twenty feet before I hit another wall. I pushed it open, walking into my bathroom, next to the sink. Luke whistled when he came through, and Jess gasped. "My mom decided that I needed a secret passageway to a couple rooms in the house in case of emergencies."

"What kind of emergency would you need to get to the bathroom for?" Luke asked, grinning devilishly.

"Obviously for when I'm being held hostage and need to pee," I responded, laughing at the scandalized look on Jess's face.

"Well, I need to shower," Jess said, after the last of Luke and my chuckles died down, "so get out."

"Gladly," Luke said, dragging me back through the hidden door, only letting go so we wouldn't hit our heads on the sloping walls. When we got back into my room, I sat back down on my bed, surprised when Luke dropped down next to me. He yawned and lay down, shifting closer to me when I used his chest as a pillow. He wrapped his arms around me, staring up at my light. I squirmed, trying to find a comfortable position on his six-pack, finally giving up and pushing off him into a vertical position. I crossed my legs and poked him until he sat up too. "Was that necessary?" He yawned again. "I'm tired."

"Same," I said, my jaw cracking.

"At least you'll get to catch up on your sleep in a month," he said and grinned, poking my cheek with his pointer finger. I stuck my tongue out at him and punched his arm lightly.

"Riley," he gasped, clutching his arm dramatically, "you wound me."

"Good." I laughed, raising my arm to hit him again. He caught my wrist and twisted my arm lightly so I was hitting myself in the head.

"Why are you hitting yourself?" he taunted like a five-year old. I was breathless, gasping for air, not realizing how close my face was to his until he touched my cheek gently and closed the one-inch gap to brush his lips with mine. An electric shock of surprise shot through me, my toes curling. He leaned in again, pressing his lips to mine with more substance than before, and I responded immediately. My hands went up to his face, framing his cheeks, and he drew one arm around me, pulling me closer. His lips moved quickly against mine, prying mine open sweetly. I brushed my tongue against his bottom lip, releasing a draft of air from him. I tilted farther into him, my mind blissfully blank until we both came up for air. I could feel my face pulsing with heat; he had two symmetrical spots of heat in line with his nose. We stared openly at each other for a minute, catching our breath.

"Luke, I can't," I started, trying to figure out how to say how much I wished he had done this sooner. His face hardened before I could continue.

"I get it," he said, with a brave smile. "We're just friends."

"No, that's not what I meant," I said, reaching for him when he got off my bed and strode to the door.

"I get it," he said, in an achingly sad voice that crushed the still beating parts of my heart.

Chapter Six

uke," I called after him, but he was already gone and I was alone. I got dressed for bed, wiping off my makeup dully and lying down on my bed; the warm spot where Luke had been sitting was cooling, and I curled into it. I pretended to be asleep when Jess came back wearing a towel. She got changed, taking a spare sleeping bag out of my closet and turning off the light.

"Goodnight," she said, mostly to herself. At eleven, my mom came to check on us, turning on the light. I kept my eyes closed, even though she had woken me up from the daze I had entered. Jess must have been asleep by then too because my mom turned off the light and left a minute later.

I woke up the next morning feeling more optimistic than I had before. It was Friday; nothing could go wrong on a Friday, right? Jess and I took turns in the bathroom, leaving thirty minutes earlier than usual to avoid my mom and Alex. We bought breakfast in the cafeteria and coffee and sat in the picnic area of the courtyard, despite the freezing temperature. I couldn't feel my fingers wrapped around the coffee, but on the plus side, Jess told me that she'd never seen me with that much color in my face. "Why are you guys out here?" Luke asked when he had finally tracked us down.

"We had to eat breakfast, and we can't eat in the hallways," Jess answered, crumpling up the wrapper to her egg and cheese sandwich, throwing it away. I rolled my eyes over her head at Luke and he returned my grin. I actually thought I was going to fly away from happiness; Luke and I were back to normal.

40

I drifted through the normal classes, waking up for lunch then going back into my brain-dead state until the ending bell. Luke held my bag for me while I put the books I needed into it, joking with him about our surprising lack of homework. Jess finally joined us and we started our trek to Luke's house, since it was Friday, before I remembered my phone. "Shit," I cried, hitting myself in the forehead.

"What?" Luke inquired, taking my arm before I could hit myself again.

"I forgot my phone." I sighed, turning back and retracing my steps to the school. It was completely empty when we got inside. I took the shortcut to my chemistry classroom, walking quickly. When we reached it, I turned into the doorway and almost ran over Sterling who was walking out.

"Watch it, bitch," she snapped (admittedly, I liked the nickname "bitch" more than I liked "princess").

"I know you don't have friends, but what are you doing in school on a Friday afternoon?" I frowned, interested in what she could possibly be doing in my classroom if she didn't even take the subject.

"None of your business," she retorted, pushing past me. "Hey, Luke." She smiled, batting her eyelashes, before she turned a corner and was gone.

"That was weird, right?" I said, staring after her.

"Maybe she wanted to see what an advanced classroom looked like," Luke suggested, giving me a little push towards the open door. "Come on, let's get your phone so we can go home." My teacher was nowhere to be found, but my phone was on the desk with a sticker that said *Riley*, so I took it and we all left together. Luke must have warned his mom about my circumstances because when we arrived there was already a steaming pot of mashed potatoes on the stove with gravy bubbling next to it.

"I love your mom." I sighed blissfully, inhaling the aroma of comfort food.

"Same," Jess agreed, moving towards the stove.

"I third that," Luke nodded lovingly.

"Hey kids," the object of our affection said, walking into the kitchen. "I heard you needed some comfort," she added, looking at me.

41

"Thanks, Mrs. Moore." I smiled, resisting the compulsion to curl up in a ball on the ground and cry into my mashed potatoes.

"Is he cute at least?" she asked in a conspiratorial whisper.

I nodded behind Luke's back while he yelled, "Mom!" at her.

"That's good," she said sadly, handing me a bowl of mashed potatoes. "Gravy?"

"Please," I said, laughing at her much-too-empathetic expression.

"We're going to my room," Luke told her after we'd all gotten bowls of homemade potatoes.

"I'd say keep the door open, but I think Riley and Jess's judgment is too good to have a threesome so do whatever you want," she replied, grinning at us and then at Luke's deep frown.

"Thanks, mom." Jess and I gave her thumbs ups while climbing the stairs and Luke turned his grimace on us and sighed. "I'm out numbered." We sat on his floor in a circle, eating our food in silence.

"No research today?" Jess finally asked, breaking the quiet gently.

"What's the point?" I said, biting my lip before it could tremble and give me away.

"So you're just going to give up?" Luke snapped, and I looked at him in surprise. "It's your life, Rye. Don't let them do this."

"It's not my life, Luke," I retorted, a sob shattering my throat before I could stop it. He put his potatoes on the ground and took my face in his hands, forcing me to look at him. A single tear trickled down my face and he wiped it away lightly. "I'm not letting them do anything," I said softly so he wouldn't hear my voice crack. "It's not my choice."

"Don't worry, sweetie," Jess cut in, wrapping her arm around me, "we'll be in that room with you. We'll follow you around for the entire day until you're so sick of us that you want to throw yourself on the thorns."

"Thanks." I laughed, two more tears escaping as I blinked.

"You're welcome," she answered, kissing the top of my head. "I need more food, you want any?"

"I'm good," I said, gesturing to my nearly full bowl. She unfolded herself gracefully from the floor and headed back downstairs. When we couldn't hear her footsteps anymore, Luke looked back at me, rubbing the tears off my face with his sleeve.

"I'd say I'm sorry about yesterday, but I'm not," he said finally, after a minute of awkward eye contact.

"Me neither," I decided. I wasn't, but it could have happened sooner for my taste. He gave me a surprised look.

"You're not?"

"Of course not," I said shrugging, "but I can't do anything about it, because I only have a month of freedom left, and we all know my mom's going to make me date Alex."

"I don't care," he murmured, leaning forward towards me. "I can take Alex, and a month is better than nothing, right?"

"I guess," I said, glancing at the door. When I turned my head back, he was so close that I could smell his minty aftershave. "I don't," I started, his lips cutting me off. I threaded my fingers through his brown hair, tilting my head into him.

"Told you so," Jess said cheerfully. We broke apart suddenly, Luke rubbing his lip where I had bitten down in surprise; I blushed so deeply I'm surprised a blood vessel didn't pop.

"Told me what?" I grumbled, shooting Luke an apologetic look that he dismissed with a wave of his hand.

"That he liked you!" Jess giggled.

"Wait, was there any doubt?" Luke asked, shaking his head. "I wasn't even subtle; I tried to kiss you in school."

"I thought you were joking," I said defensively, ignoring the little shriek that Jess had uttered.

"And I come to your locker every single morning. You know I wasn't there for Jess, right?"

"Hey!" Jess said, trying to be grouchy but failing to conceal a wide smile.

"Rude," I grinned.

"I know, right?" he said, taking my face again and kissing me in a slow (but building, I promise) kiss.

"No more," Jess begged, her nose wrinkled at us.

"Sorry," I said, pulling away.

"I'm not," Luke smirked.

We did end up doing research after all. Mrs. Moore brought us food at around six (she really was the best), actual food this time not mashed potatoes, and sat down to join us. "Hand me a book," she told Luke, who stared blankly at her with his mouth open. "Book," she repeated, pointing to the *Curses of History* book lying next to him (yes they really have one of those; you'd be surprised what you can find on Amazon).

"You're going to help?" he asked uncomprehendingly. I reached over and closed his jaw gently with a click.

"Of course," she said, the "duh" vibrating through each syllable. "I want to keep Riley as much as you do."

"Thanks, Mrs. Moore," I beamed, blowing her a kiss. "But I think people wanting to keep me might be part of the problem."

"Don't worry," she said, smiling gently, "I actually love you enough to let you go."

"Damn it," I said laughing through a watery grin, "I thought I was done with crying."

"Don't cry!" she begged jokingly, "I can't make any more mashed potatoes or my fingers will fall off."

"I love your mom," I said to Luke, and with that we read our books in a happy silence. I flipped through the index in my book on black curses until I found the *Sleeping Beauty Curse* under the S section. I skimmed it briefly, but there was nothing new. It had the same basic factors:

- *One person starting the curse, and having it carry through the family until one generation broke it for good*
- *Prince*
- *Kissing*
- *Hundred year sleep unless 'true love' finds her first*
- *Thorns*
- *Fairy godmother (Which I definitely needed)*

"Anything yet?" Luke asked, poking my face when I zoned out, staring at the book and not taking anything in.

"Same as always," I said, focusing back to the page which was looking considerably blurrier than it had.

"This one says that if you sacrifice your soul to Satan you have a fifty-percent chance of not having a spell cast on you because the spell only works on the pure," Jess said looking up from her research.

"No," Mrs. Moore said when I opened my mouth.

"I was just going to say that it was tempting," I grumbled at her.

"Is that a no?" Jess asked, hesitating on the page.

"Of course that's a no!" Mrs. Moore frowned.

"Fine," I muttered, closing my book and reaching for a different one.

After another three hours, we had given up completely and decided to watch the Disney version of *Sleeping Beauty*, Luke and I making fun (not making out for those of you that have dirty minds and misread what I said) of the princes and the way the Princess woke up, and Mrs. Moore and Jess shushing us every five seconds. I left for my house at around one, Luke insisting on walking me home. I refused politely, wanting to be alone. I took my time walking down the frosted sidewalks, my breath coming out as vapor.

I was a block away from my house when I heard a weird sound behind me. I whipped around, but no one was there. I picked up my pace (yes I know you're visualizing this as the beginning of every horror movie ever) and stopping abruptly when I heard the noise again. I hesitated, wanting to explore what was behind me, and having watched too many slasher films to be as dumb as all the main characters in those. I walked backwards now, watching the bushes where I thought I had seen movement, but now the sound came from behind me, which had been in front of me. I ran the rest of the way home without looking back, chills jetting through my body when I heard the gasping rustles moving just as quickly as me. I sprinted through my front door, closing it quietly but quickly. I could have sworn that I heard something slam into it behind me, but when I looked out the front windows there was nothing but grass sparkling in the moonlight. I shivered in my uniform, teeth chattering until I took a steaming hot shower. I layered the blankets on my bed until I was cocooned, taking one last look out of my window before pulling down the shades and falling asleep.

When I woke up in the morning, it was early. I got up, got a drink of water and fell back asleep. The second time, I could feel the sun streaming through the gaps in my curtains, turning my eyelids red. I rolled over slightly, and the sunlight was cut off by a large shadow. I opened one of my eyes blearily. My mom was standing in front of me with her arms crossed, glaring down at me. "Do you know what time it is?" she snapped.

"Well, if you moved I would be able to see my clock," I replied, yawning and stretching, less than elegantly. I heard a distinctly masculine chuckle come from behind her, and I craned my neck to see. Alex was leaning against my wall, surveying me with amusement. "Lovely," I grumbled, rolling back over and burying my head under my pillow. I felt the pillow being ripped off of my face at the same time that my blanket was pulled off my body. I ignored them both, curling up into a ball instead. My mom cleared her throat and I heard Alex give a short cough of laugh again. I had an image of my mom pretending not to frown, but her forehead creasing anyway, holding my bedding hostage.

"It's nine in the morning," she snapped.

"That's it?" I said, arching an eyebrow while keeping my eyes closed.

"Alex," she said, voice sweetening, "can you give us a second?"

"Ok," he said, still trying not to laugh. I heard receding footsteps until I could tell we were alone. After a short intermission of silence, I opened my eyes fully. She was still standing there, not even pretending to hide her grimace at me anymore.

"What?" I frowned, rubbing my eyes.

"Get up," she hissed at me, glancing around in case Alex was still somewhere in the ten-mile vicinity.

"Why?" I groaned. It was only nine; why did my mom have to do this.

"You have a date," she snapped. That woke me up in a hurry.

"No I don't," I replied, rolling over again. She grabbed my arm and tried to pull me out of bed, which only succeeded in creating a permanent handprint on my wrist. All the beauty sleep had made her weak (especially in the brain).

"Yes, you do," she answered, rummaging through my drawers and pulling out clothes. She held up a skirt and tank top combo, shook her head and pulled out a dress. She threw it on top of me and shook my shoulders again.

"No." I frowned, glaring at the dress, but I got up.

Ten minutes later I had been bribed (she offered me no curfew, which I accepted of course. I may have high morals but freedom was freedom), threatened (she tried to take away the curfew when I refused the dress again. I wore the dress), primped (she decided that my naturally straight hair needed to be straightened) and made up (my eyes were so sticky with mascara that I had to fight to keep them open every time I blinked). The dress she had picked out was short, strapless, and provided absolutely no warmth; "You know it's December, right?" I asked rhetorically, as she circled me, admiring her work.

"Wear a coat." She shrugged. Solid parenting. Thankfully for me, a few snowflakes fluttered down outside and she changed her mind, forcing me into a tightly low-cut sweater and leggings instead. I had to admit that I did look good; too bad that I was going on a date with the wrong boy. I bit my lip as she added brushes of foundation to my face and neck, wondering what Luke would say if he could see me looking like a girl. Wait, *Luke*. I glanced at my bed where my phone was sitting, taunting me. "I think that's enough," she said finally, standing back to admire her work.

"Looks good," I said, grabbing my phone and leaving the room. I grabbed a coat from the hall closet, and a pair of my fuzzy (and admittedly, ugly) boots.

"No, no, no," she called after me, intercepting me before I could walk into the living room where I could hear my dad and Alex talking. She handed me a pair of heels, the same silvery gray as my sweater. I opened my mouth to argue, but she raised her eyebrows warningly in a way that clearly screamed, *Curfew?*

"Fine," I grumbled, pulling them on. It was like having wild animals trying to eat my toes on my feet, which magically made me five inches taller.

"Riley's ready," my mom exclaimed, waltzing into the living room. I smiled at Alex from behind her, my other hand on my phone shielded from view by my mother where no one else could see. *911, first date with Alex today, send help*, I texted to Luke, hoping he would pass the news on to Jess too.

47

"So where do you want to go?" Alex asked when we finally made it out of the house, after hundreds of pictures taken by my parents ("You'll have these to show to your kids," they had said, making us pose like we were going to prom). I shrugged and avoided eye contact.

"Wherever."

"Well, I don't know this town," he said good-naturedly. I saw him reach for my hand out of the corner of my eye and quickly shoved it deep into my coat pockets. I felt my phone buzz under where my hand was hiding from his. I pulled it out, checking it even though I could feel him watching me. *Where??????* Luke had replied. I swapped the phone to my other hand so Alex couldn't see what I had written.

"How about Starbucks?" I smiled at him, while I texted the same thing to Luke.

The Starbucks in Racheston was inside the huge central bookstore, which in turn was inside of a mansion (what else; it's Racheston). I got us a seat in the cozy stuffed couches side by side in an alcove containing the fireplace, where I could watch out of the second story windows for my salvation. He walked back downstairs to get us coffees, returning a few minutes later. "Thanks," I smiled politely, accepting the latte.

"You're welcome," he said, sitting down on my couch, uncomfortably close. I shifted away from him, but he followed my movements until I was near the armrest at the end of it. He yawned, stretching his arm until it was around my shoulders. Classic white boy pickup move.

"Nice," I said, shaking my head at him.

"What?" he asked, looking confused, but I could see the glitter in his eyes.

He ran his fingers through his swoopy (can't believe that's a word but I didn't know how else to describe it, sorry) blonde hair, flicking his bangs to the side. His eyes were brown; the wrong color for me. I had expected them to look warm and comforting up close, but instead they looked like mud that had been frozen over and had never quite thawed. They unsettled me, and I moved closer to the armrest, breaking eye contact. I took a light sip of my coffee, scalding my tongue and making me cringe. When I looked back up, he was ten times closer, leaning towards my mouth.

"Whoa," I said, putting one hand on his chest and pushing, hard.

"I thought we could practice," he smirked, tongue running over his lips, "for your birthday." I was stuck against the armrest, his arm encircling me so I was trapped.

"No thanks," I said, squirming against his grasp, which only made him hold on tighter. His eyes flashed angrily and he forced his lips onto mine. I felt such a sudden shock down my spine that it was almost painful, and I resisted his lips furiously. They moved roughly against mine and something snapped inside me. I opened my eyes, lacing my fingers through his hair and yanking his head back. His hands were around my waist, braced against my efforts.

"Hey!" I heard someone say furiously behind me, but before Luke had a chance to do anything I had brought my hand back and closed it into a fist before slamming it into Alex's stomach. He broke away, doubling over with a groan. I drew my hand back again, punching him in the face this time.

"Bitch," he gasped, crouched over and spitting out blood.

Chapter Seven

Next time, when I say no kissing me, don't kiss me," I snapped. "I'm not a bitch; you're just a self-indulgent asshole who expects me to fall all over him." I stood up, and Jess caught my eye with a grin.

"You're lucky she's the one who hit you," Luke said calmly, standing over the still wheezing Alex, "because if I had done it, you wouldn't have a nose right now."

"Are you saying that I hit like a girl?" I frowned at him.

"Obviously not," he replied. "It looks like Alex is down a tooth now. Sorry we came so late. Jess wanted a pumpkin spice latte and we thought you would be okay for an extra five minutes."

"Thanks," I said, rolling my eyes at Jess who sipped her latte innocently.

"We were right," she defended. "You've proven that you can." Luke and I laughed, and he wrapped his arms around me, ignoring the hiss from Alex. He bent his head down but I flinched backwards.

"I think that's enough kissing for me today," I said, glaring at Alex who had a trickle of bloody saliva dripping from the corner of his mouth. Between his icy white skin and light hair (and most importantly his bloody mouth) he looked like a vampire straight out a romance novel.

"Whatever," Alex said, shoving violently past us, taking the stairs two at a time before he disappeared from view. We looked at each other and cracked up, breathlessly collapsing on couches. Luke finally noticed my bruised knuckles and took my hand in both of his, gently running his fingers over the cracks.

"Let's go get your hands fixed up," he suggested. I agreed, and we left for his house, stopping briefly to buy me more coffee (I didn't have the stomach to drink the one from Alex).

His mom gasped when she saw my bruised hand, and ran to get a first age kit from the bathroom. "Do I want to know what happened?" she asked finally, after my hand was wrapped in gauze and she had given me an ice pack to put on it.

"Someone tried to kiss me," I answered shortly. She gave Luke a quick look up and down.

"I don't see any bruises on my son," she teased.

"Mom!" He frowned at her, and then at Jess and me when we started giggling.

"It was someone else that I barely knew," I gasped, still laughing at Luke's indignation.

"Oh, Alex?" she assumed.

"I see you and Luke talk more than my mom and I do." I frowned at him. He gave me a contrite look and a peck on the cheek.

"Sorry," she mouthed at him. "So, he tried to kiss you?"

"And I said no, and he did it anyway so I punched him," I filled in for her.

"Hell yes," she said, grinning and giving me a high five. We all looked at her in scandalized shock. "What, just because I'm old I'm not allowed to swear?" she said. "Close your mouths, you'll catch flies," she added, standing up from where we were sitting on the floor and putting the first aid kit back upstairs.

"God, I love your mom," I said, leaning back to rest against his couch.

"Same," Jess agreed, mimicking my relaxed expression.

"I third that," Luke decided, pulling me into his chest and enclosing me in his arms.

"Can I fourth that?" his mom queried coming back and sitting down with us. We chuckled lightly at that and she gave a little bow.

"Why do you live in Racheston?" I asked suddenly, when Jess and Mrs. Moore had just started talking about the weather.

"What?" she said, in surprised amusement.

"It's just," I struggled to make it sound as least insulting as I could, "everyone here is so—happy all of the time." *There we go, Riley. That won't insult her at all.*

"I'm happy," she said, affronted.

"But you're real happy," I said, clarifying, "you're not 'happy housewives' happy, where they all pretend to like their lives but they're really just empty shells, trying to seem the most cultured and stuck up even though this is Massachusetts. Everyone here is fake and sexist and expects girls to be perfect and ladylike, and boys to be dashing and controlling and in the meantime we all just want to run as far away as we can but we can't because money is a more powerful factor than feelings so we swallow our feelings again and again until finally we have nothing left but scrapbooking and designer purses that our husbands will love," I finished, gasping for air after the longest run on sentence ever. She looked thoughtfully overwhelmed, and studied me for a while before replying.

"All the 'happy housewives' were raised to be submissive because money means doing what your parents tell you to, and they were pushed down and controlled until they finally broke. But I met my husband in college, and fell in love before I even knew he was rich or lived in this town, so I didn't need to be 'happy' all the time or need the money. And I was raised by my successful single mom, so she was the example to show me that I didn't need a husband or money to live a good life, but it she also taught me that I didn't have to live on my own completely independent either," she said. "And I don't think we need to worry about you either because if you were planning on being a 'happy housewife' you wouldn't have your hand bandaged."

"But how do I know I won't want to be a 'happy housewife' in the near future?" I cried, unsatisfied by her answer. She was raised to be independent, but my mom told me almost every day that my life goal should be to find a man to take care of me.

"I think you're safe," she answered, laughing for some reason. "Riley, your parents aren't going to be happy if you're not a 'happy housewife' but you'll never be happy as one and you know it. Your personality's a little strong to succumb to the fairytales, don't you think?"

"I think so," Luke said, kissing the top of my head.

"We all know you're safe from that," Jess added, taking my hand. "I think Alex is the one that should be worried. You're in more danger of murdering him in his sleep or eloping with Luke than you are of cooking healthy dinners and having ten kids and *scrapbooking*."

"Eloping is not a bad idea," Luke nodded wisely. "They can't marry you off if you're already married, right?"

"Thanks," I said, rolling my eyes with so much velocity that I gave myself a headache, "when I want to avoid getting married at a young age by getting married at a young age then I'll give you a call."

"I better be the first person that you call," he threatened jokingly.

"Actually," I said, pausing to think about it, "Jess will be the first person that I call. It's legal in Massachusetts, right?"

"Sorry, Riley, but I don't feel that way about you," she said, withdrawing her hand. "Not that there's anything wrong with that," she included, glancing around like she was worried someone had witnessed her brief moment of not being completely and clearly kind to every person in the entire world. I exchanged a grin with Luke who knew, at least, that I was joking.

"I feel like this has been enough of a heart to heart." Mrs. Moore laughed, standing up and moving towards the kitchen. "Who wants dinner?"

"Me!" I said, Luke helping me off the floor.

"Me too," Jess called, taking longer to get up since she didn't have anyone to help her.

"What do you want?"

"Pizza!" we all cried in unison, childlike in its harmony.

"Deal," she said, "since I don't really want to cook anyway." She dialed the number for the local pizza place. "What do you want?" she mouthed while it rang.

"Bacon," Luke said while I said "pineapple" and Jessica said "plain". She sighed and shook her head at us, holding the phone back up to her ear when we heard the click of someone picking up.

"One large pizza with a quarter bacon, half plain and a quarter pineapple," she said. She listened while the person kept talking, throwing out the occasional "no thank you" and saying "delivery" and their address before hanging up. "Couldn't have made it easy, could you," she said shaking her head fondly.

"Never," we concurred together.

"Course not," she said. "Thirty minutes before the pizza comes they said, or it's free." We headed up to Luke's room to get some research done before dinner, but we ended up hanging out on his bed, just talking. I leaned against his wall, my feet hanging off the short side of his bed, Luke next to me, and Jess on the diagonal, leaning against his headboard. I felt a pang when I realized how much I was going to miss them when I was married and having kids and they were off at college (cheesy, I know) and my eyes welled up with tears, one escaping to trickle down my cheek. Jess stopped telling us a story about how she had gotten a B up to an A when she was talking to her English teacher and stared blankly at me.

"I know that Jess's story was moving and everything," Luke said, reaching an arm around my shoulders, "but are you okay?"

"No." I sniffled. "We only have another month of this, and then you guys get to have a life and I'm going to be stuck here."

"We'll never let that happen!" Jess cried angrily. "We'll kidnap you if we have to, and move to Europe and change our names before we let you stay here all alone." Luke nodded fervently, kissing me squarely on my mouth before Jess made a gagging sound.

"Thanks," I said, wiping my eyes, "but I don't think you'll actually be able to do anything about this extremely crappy situation. I shouldn't have even made friends. I should have just eaten lunch in the school bathroom and not talked to anyone in class and sat at the back."

"I had a huge crush on you in freshmen year, I don't think any of that would have discouraged me," Luke said, running his hands through his hair.

"Wait, *had* a crush?" I frowned, momentarily distracted from the future to focus on the present.

"Sorry, I *have* a huge crush on you," he said, abashed.

"Nice slip," Jess grinned at him while he flushed a deeper color.

"Wow," I said, shaking my head in mock hurt. "I never expected this from you Lucas Moore."

"I'm sorry," he repeated, kissing the palm of my hand, and then the top of it, making his way slowly up my arm to my neck.

"God," Jess said wrinkling her nose in distaste, "can you at least *try* and hide your cuteness, you disgusting people."

"Never," Luke murmured against the skin under my ear. I giggled when his lips tickled my cheek, and Jess threw a pillow at me.

"Pizza's here," Mrs. Moore yelled up the stairs, interrupting what was doomed to become a full-fledged pillow fight.

"This isn't over, Jessica," Luke hissed cheerfully through his teeth.

"I think we all know that I would have won," she replied cheekily, and he glared at her.

"Guess we'll never know." I shrugged and they both turned on me. "Sorry," I muttered, holding my hands up in surrender. I was ahead of both of the bickering children behind me, grabbing two pieces of my pineapple pizza and joining Mrs. Moore on the couch.

"Let's watch a different movie than *Sleeping Beauty*," she suggested, flicking through the channels. "There is," she went through the guide, "*Jaws*, *A Cinderella Story* and *Die Hard*. People dying, romance, or people dying with a slight romantic subplot?'

"People dying with a slight romantic subplot please," I answered, taking a bite of pizza. She turned on *Die Hard* and a few seconds later, Jess and Luke came in, still arguing about the pillow fight. I shushed them and watched Bruce Willis crawling through air ducts. I fell asleep after *Die Hard* when Mrs. Moore and Jess decided to watch *The Little Mermaid*, my head in Luke's lap.

When I woke up, their house was dark and quiet. I rolled over, surprised when I didn't fall off the couch onto the floor. I opened my eyes fully and looked around, before closing them again. I was just in their spare guest bedroom; wait, bedroom? My eyes flew open and I checked the clock on the shelf in front of me. Four-thirty AM is what it claimed in glowing numbers. Since I didn't have a curfew anymore, who cared? I rolled over and went back to sleep. I woke up again to someone poking my face. "What," I grumbled into the pillow.

"Come on, princess." Luke laughed, stroking my hair, which I was sure was a tangled mess. "You'll have plenty of time to sleep in a month."

"Asshole," I muttered, squinting at him.

"That's me. Come on, your mom has called our house twenty

times."

"Another good reason for me to stay in bed," I said decidedly, curling up under their comforter. He tried to teasingly lift me out of bed, but only succeeded in falling on top of me when I pulled on his arm.

"Oof," he said, his face muffled in a pillow.

"This is not what I sent you up here for," I heard Mrs. Moore say from the doorway. I looked over and she was smirking good-naturedly. "Come on, Riley, I'll walk you home."

"You don't have to do that, really," I said, pushing Luke off the bed and climbing over him. I was still fully clothed (that's always good?) and my shoes were by the door. I hesitated before slipping them on; they really were incredibly uncomfortable.

"Nonsense," she replied, looping her arm through mine.

"We're off to see the wizard," I sang under my breath when Luke took my other arm.

"Sounds like a code for drugs," Luke observed, his mom reaching across me to hit him lightly.

"If we're going to see my mom I might need some," I said as Luke held the front door for me and shut it behind us.

He pinched his thumb against his nostril and pretended to snort something off of it. "I think I just found my brain," he joked, shaking his head. I laughed in a short burst of surprise while Mrs. Moore shook her head disapprovingly.

"We don't need drugs," she said, frowning at Luke. "If we all show up together then her anger will be separated and no one person will get the brunt of it."

"Hugs, not drugs," Luke agreed, nodding wisely.

"Says the people who have their own house and can leave after getting a portion of her crazy," I grumbled, but smiled all the same. At least someone had my back, since I'm assuming my dad would be cowering ("working") at the office, even though it was Sunday.

Chapter Eight

I searched through my pockets when we neared my house, but no key surfaced. "Guess we're ringing the doorbell." I shrugged, and they nodded. I pressed the doorbell, listening to the echo reverberating through the cold halls of the mansion. My mom pulled it open violently before I had a chance to press it again.

"Oh, good, you're home," she said distractedly, ushering me and my posse in and shutting the door, leaning against it.

"Are you okay?" I asked, feeling her forehead. She looked like she was on the verge of a mental breakdown. She threw out a politely brave smile, and nodded.

"Your grandmother decided that she wanted to visit you before your big day. Only three weeks to go and everything," she replied, pushing herself off the door and fanning herself with her apron.

"The evil one?" I asked in a stage whisper. I had never met my grandmother but if she made my mom this anxious then damn if this wasn't going to be a good three weeks.

"Evil?" came an annoyed voice from behind me. "Is that how you're describing me these days, Rose?" I turned around to witness a four-foot tall woman, with a back as straight as a ramrod and piercing blue eyes. She radiated power, even with her strictly adorable height, and I could see my mom shrinking away out of the corner of my eye. Then my grandma turned to me and winked; I could feel the edges of my lips curling up at the edges. "At least someone in this family says what she's thinking," she added approvingly. My mom excused herself, and practically ran back into the kitchen. "So who are you people?" grandma asked, directing her intimidating attention at the Moores.

"I'm a friend of Riley," Mrs. Moore said, holding out her hand.

"And you?" the old woman asked, turning to Luke.

He glanced at me before introducing himself. "It's complicated, but I'd like to think that I'm Riley's boyfriend."

"Complicated, hmm?" she said with a knowing smile at me. "What's complicated is the swollen lip and fractured nose that you gave your prince, dear."

"That's not complicated," I snorted derisively. "When I say no kissing, I mean no kissing." I expected my mom's stepmom to scold me, or send me a disappointed look, but instead her grin widened.

"It's a miracle that you've resisted your mom's genes so well," she said proudly. "Lady-like my ass."

"Evil my ass," I countered, feeling my insides melt (in a good way, not in a life-threatening way) when she gave me another pleased smile.

"We have a lot to catch up on," she said, leading me over to the couch, which the Moores took as their cue to leave, motioning apologetically. "So," she started, examining me, "what has your mom told you about me?"

"Just that you were evil and didn't like my dad," I answered.

"Oh, I liked your father well enough," she said, waving her hand dismissively. "I just thought that they were too young to get married. They were only eighteen after all."

"I've been waiting for so long for someone in my family to say that," I said, relaxing against the couch.

"Sorry, doll," she said, patting my cheek, "but I'm not technically related to you. None of my genes are actually in you."

"Don't say that," I moaned, covering my face with my hands. "So why does my mom hate you?" I asked, changing the subject sloppily. I needed to work on my transitions.

She shrugged, looking towards the kitchen and then back at me. "I never understood her fascination with princesses and her curse until after it had happened. She was always distant and I didn't try as hard as I should have, and then she blamed me for the curse and it was all over."

"How can she blame you for a curse that has been in my family for hundreds of years?"

"You're wondering how your mother could be difficult and unreasonable?" she said, giving me another piercing old-lady look.

"Point taken," I said. She started to say something else, but my mom came out of the kitchen with a tray of cookies. I reached for one but she slapped my hand away.

"Not for you, dear. Can't get fat before your big day." She smiled. I looked down at my flat and empty stomach that growled its disapproval.

"I'm sure I'll burn off some calories while I'm asleep, metabolism and all that," I said, reaching for one again. She relented, but the corner of her mouth turned down when I tried to take two. I sighed and replaced the second one. I took a big bite, closing my eyes when it melted in my mouth. There was no way I was ever going to make cookies this delicately mouth-watering. I didn't have the attention span anyway.

"When are you planning on apologizing to Alex?" my mom asked with unforced nonchalance, like she was planning on marking it in her calendar.

"On the thirtieth of February," I answered, stealing another cookie before she could stop me.

"Why so late?" She frowned, completely missing the point. I exchanged a look with my grandma; at least she had understood. She was suppressing a smile, hiding short laughs in coughs.

"I'm sorry," I said, not even bothering to hide the snap in my voice, "I meant never."

"Riley Ivory Owens," she said in a harsh whisper. She dragged me off the couch and into an adjoining room, shutting the door with a quiet click. "What is your problem with Alex?" she said, keeping her voice at a low level so that my grandma wouldn't hear and come join the side of feminism.

"Besides the fact that he forced himself on me?" I cried, ignoring her desperate shushing. I expected her to take my side, to say something like "he did what?" and storm his room to kick him out but not surprisingly, she brushed away that information.

"I'm sure he was just making sure that your kiss would be perfect on your birthday," she said defensively. "You broke his nose Riley. An apology *is* in order."

I stared at her with a chill that should have frozen her solid. I imagined the frost sliding over her toes, up her legs until she was ice; she would be so nice and quiet as ice. We could keep her in the freezer, and she would be equally as chilly and beautiful as she was now.

"Make me," I said, staring her down with a barely insinuated threat. I recoiled when her manicured fingers hit my face, tears springing to my eyes and rolling down my cheeks as I ran, not looking back.

"Riley," she yelled after me, but I was already out the door.

I started to drift in the direction of Luke's house, but he had seen me cry enough for one week. I circled the house instead, walking towards the long stretch of woods behind it. Our property bordered the only real forest(ish) reserve in Racheston, which ended at a small marsh near the ocean that in turn led into a rocky public beach. This time of year, it would be deserted, so I started heading in the general way that I thought it would be. I had to duck under the low hanging branches, broken from the snow that we had gotten in November. They had held pounds of snow, but when the weight was lifted they had refused to spring back, choosing instead to hang at broken angles. The healthier trees had been forced to stay that way, by gravity or the breaks in the elbows of them.

I could see the water sparkling ahead of me (after about an hour of walking; I'm a slow walker), despite the cloudy day. The trees, formerly so close together that I had turned sideways to slip through, were starting to thin out, and I started seeing footprints where people had travelled through, but refused to go any deeper. I pushed through the last remaining branches and stepped out onto the beach. I loved our beach. It had almost no sand, considering how calm the water always was; it was like being on a lake, perfect for families but not so great if you wanted to surf. The ground was a scattering of littler rocks on top of the huge slabs of natural granite that made up the ground. The earth slowly sloped up, so that if you walked far enough along it, you could end up a few feet above the water where the tide pools were.

Tall cliffs, jutting dramatically out of the still water, marked the end of the beach; these were my destination. There was one 'father' cliff where a few mansions sat, and my rocks were more like columns, barely attached to anything. Some were only held in place by sheer gravity, and leaned to dangerous angles (don't worry I avoid those). With practiced hands, I scaled the first rock, only about twenty feet high. It was attached to a steeply narrow ledge, made by erosion cut into the "father" cliff and clean from any tread marks. No one else dared to come up here.

I guided my way with a hand grasping at natural handholds, treading gently, one foot directly in front of the other. I got to a rock about waist high and lifted myself onto it. The rest of the rocks were like stairs, and I climbed by jumping over the gaps where the tide crawled slowly over land before retreating with a hiss. I finally stopped on my favorite one. It had been cut out in a shape at the edges so that it looked almost like a chair, the half facing the ocean lower than the side closer to land. I settled into it, wiping the remnants of my nearly frozen tears on the back of my hand. After a while of staring at the horizon, I shifted my position so that I could see all the way down into the water. It was close enough to the shore that it was almost clear, and I could see fish skirting the rocks and flicking away. I propped my head up on my arms and stared at them until their careful dance with the tide lulled me to sleep.

I woke up stiff and cold, the sun painting a spray of pink and gold through the clouds. "Crap," I muttered, looking to the ground. I had never been in the forest after dark, as my parents had forbidden it, probably worried that I would go to live with the owls and never come back. If it was dark when I got there, the odds of me being able to find my way through was highly doubtful. Plus, I tripped on the roots in full daylight with no handicap to my vision. I would probably break my legs if I was trying to scramble over them with just the moonlight to guide me. Climbing down proved more challenging than going up. By the time I was on solid land, my hands were scraped and bleeding and my chin had a bruise blooming from when my foot had slipped. I guess if I had died my mom would have felt bad about her last words to me, but I wasn't willing to go that far for revenge. Not that I'm a nice person; I'd just rather see her face when I ultimately counter-attacked. I tried to rub feeling into my legs, but trekking across the rocky beach was slow going. The sun was almost completely down when I finally made it to the first of the trees.

The sun dipped down and I pulled out my phone to use as a flashlight as darkness flushed the sky. I had gotten into the last of the worn footprints when the trees started to move right in front of me. They locked branches, fortifying into a wall, and I could hear the trees behind me bending too.

I forced my arm through a gap in the quickly closing barrier, and to my surprise they stopped instead of cutting my arm off. I slid my arm down, and the gap widened until I could squeeze through. Then they slammed closed behind me, like a door that had been held against gravity for too long. I pressed the flashlight app, and the beam of light illuminated the first few feet in front of me. I started to walk, carefully avoiding the roots sticking out of the ground. Noises shuffled around me, a twig cracked on the ground behind me spurring me into a run.

I had almost made it to my yard when a hand shot out of the ground, grabbing my ankle. I screamed, stomping down with my other foot until it let go. The arm attached to it slowly began to worm its way out of the loose dirt, and I took a step back, right onto another arm, this time from a different body. They were both gray and covered in alternating scales, tiny like children (horribly scaly children, but no offense to other children with scales) but one was delicately female (or a guy that moisturized a lot) and the other had hard calluses and stubby fingers with a fair amount of knuckle hair.

I heard the breaking of dirt and sprinted toward my house, straight into another wooden wall. I bounced back, feeling a lump beginning on my forehead, kicking the trees. Nothing moved; I was trapped. I started slowly reversing, looking around for any more hands. My old friends, moisturizer and stubby thumbs were poking their heads through the dirt, sure to see me.

I picked an unaffected tree and started to climb, my breath catching in panicked gasps until the vertigo hit me and I curled up on a large branch. I was glad that I had worn my black winter coat; they would never be able to see me in the dark. I could barely make out what was happening on the ground. More heads appeared, then bodies until there was an entire clan of dragon-y children things. Their backs were twisted, spines sticking out at intense angles. They had two tufts of bristling black hair: one on their back and one on the top of their dirty heads. I couldn't see what they were doing until a fire glowed from a pile of sticks they had made, quickly evolving into a roaring bonfire as they added more fuel.

I shrank against the bark of the tree, my hope of darkness protecting me quickly fading. Their faces were slowly illuminated; I was practically hugging the tree by the time I could see them. They had cruelly hooked noses and glistening filed teeth, not bone or anything natural. It looked almost like metal, reflecting in the firelight. They were communicating in sounds that were too low for me to hear, but they had to lean into each other to get across the point. Then they sat down. In the middle of whatever weird ritual these monsters were doing, they sat down on the dirt. Lazy bums. Actually, they looked like they were waiting for someone; my arms started shaking with the dread of what could make these dragon kid things sit like it was story time. Then the ground started to shake. And then, I died.

Just kidding, it takes more than an earthquake to kill me. I did almost die though. I held onto my tree for dear life, praying to God that the branch didn't snap and send me into the arms of the creatures below (it didn't if you were wondering). The ground stopped shuddering, thankfully, but then it began to split into a chasm, parallel from where I was hiding.

I give the monsters in my town an A plus for dramatics, because the smoke that started to twist upwards from the crack really helped the whole "I'm about to die" image for me. Yet another hand shot out of the passage to hell, but it was neither stubby nor well moisturized; it *was* gigantic though. Keep in mind, I was a good thirty feet in the air, and when the full being had climbed out of the fissure he was almost to my height. I trembled against the tree, but he didn't seem to see me. Then, he began to shrink until he was only ten feet tall. The dragon children things (from this point, let's just call them goblins; "dragon children things" is kind of a mouthful) cowered at his feet, bowing continuously. Ah, goblin worshipping time. Such a fun time to be a human stuck thirty feet in the air with no plan and no safe way to go home. Looks like I wasn't sleeping tonight.

He cleared his throat in a rumble that I could hear far up in the air, and his goblin minions stopped moving. He started talking in a language that definitely wasn't English; it sounded like a crude mixture of snorts and grunts. Two of his goblin minions nodded, hurrying to their lord's aid and scurrying into the depths of the forest. The other goblins got comfortable on the ground again, while big boy (the goblin king) grunted impatiently.

Twenty minutes later, the two monster servants were back, leading a boy; my arms went numb when I recognized him with horror. Clayton Devis followed the goblins, seemingly entranced. "Come on," the goblin on the right was saying in the voice of, I shuddered, Sterling. The likeness to her voice coming out of the ugly body of the goblin made me retch, grateful that I hadn't eaten anything since this morning. "Why don't you tie yourself to the tree?" the goblin said sweetly and Clayton obeyed, his glazed eyes reflecting red in the firelight. I bit my lip, trying to think of a way to break the spell he was under without drawing attention to myself. Clayton finished the tight knot around himself and big boy grumbled his approval, poking Clayton's chest with a long finger.

The goblins danced around the rising flames, throwing their hands over their heads (I was wrong; they had three clumps of hair. Someone had to introduce them to the concept of shaving their armpits). They were chanting as Clayton slowly started to wake up into his nightmare. I ran the possibilities of saving him through my head. I had no weapon, no plan, no chance against hundreds of metal-toothed goblins and a monstrous goblin god.

I closed my eyes, curling up into a ball against the tree, blocking out all of it. I couldn't keep out the building screams of my peer or the crunch of bones at the end of it. When I thought it was safe to look again, all that was left of Clayton Devis was an empty shell of ribs with scraps of skin and the spray of blood reaching around the tree and covering the face and hands of big boy. A sob caught in my throat and I covered my mouth to keep the desperation in, tears streaming down my face in hysterical rivets. My eyes grew heavy, and when I woke back up the sun had already erased any evidence of the murder and the town had erased any memory of Clayton from their minds.

The ground looked mercifully goblin free, and the trees had spread apart so that I could see the inviting grass of my backyard. I climbed down slowly, racking my brain. As far as I could tell, nothing had happened in the clearing. There was no ash from a fire, or blood from Clayton or even disturbed dirt or footprints from big boy. I circled the spot twice, unable to find anything. The third time around, I paced closer to the tree and spotted something hidden by leaves and mushrooms. I knelt down and picked up the licked clean finger bone, the last of Clayton Devis. I pocketed it and ran all the way to my front door.

Everyone was still sleeping when I opened the door; the house was deadly silent. I crept up the stairs to my bathroom, turning the hot water all the way up on my shower, and stripping carefully. My limbs were sore from holding on to a tree all night, my arms and hands cut and scabbing from all the climbing. The bump on my forehead was sporting a purple bruise, creating a throbbing, painful headache behind my eyes. The water soothed the knots in my back and neck, side effects of sleeping thirty feet in the air. I took shuddering breaths until I couldn't anymore, falling to my knees on the tiled floor, the water drumming on my face and mixing with the tears on my face. I curled up in the fetal position against the cold walls. I stayed there long after the water had turned cold and I had gone numb. After, I started to shiver, so I stood up and turned the water off. I bundled my hair into a towel, taking the secret passageway to my room. I changed into sweatpants, falling fast asleep in my bed.

When I woke up, the sky was dark again. I stood up and stretched, the fuzzy memories from the previous night invading my head until I had to lie down again to forget. And I would have gotten away with it too if it hadn't been for my meddlesome stomach, which apparently wanted to be fed every day. Selfish bastard.

I stretched, hearing all my bones crack making me shiver. I walked slowly to the kitchen, raiding my fridge and sitting at the table to eat the pile of food I collected. I ate slowly, worrying that if I stuffed it all in my mouth any slight memory would bring it all right back up. It was only nine o'clock, but the only noise was the ticking clock on the counter. I couldn't figure out where my parents had gone, until I remembered that it was Monday, and Monday was town meeting day, where all the citizens got together and complained about idiotic stuff like water fountains. And then my brain finally made a bigger connection: I had missed school! I had kept perfect attendance for all four years of high school, and even though I was hoping to graduate that way I knew that it would be ruined after my birthday. I sighed, taking another bite of leftover chicken. I was lulled into a sense of security by the silence in my house, jumping out of my seat and onto the floor when the phone rang. "Hello?" I answered, after regaining a steady heartbeat.

"Riley?" Luke asked, relief flooding his voice. "We were so worried when you didn't show for school today!"

"Oh," I said, blushing, "I overslept. I actually just woke up twenty minutes ago."

"Wow, Sleeping Beauty, save all that for next month," he teased, sounding much more relaxed.

"Sure," I muttered distractedly.

"Is everything okay?" Luke said, projecting worried syllables that rang in my ears.

"No," I said, running my hands through my hair even though he couldn't see me.

"I'll be right over," he said seriously, hanging up with a click. I tracked down a hairbrush and sat on the couch to wait for him.

The first thing he did when I opened the door for him was collect me into a hug in his arms, before stepping back. "What the hell happened to you?" he cried, rubbing his thumb gently against my bruised forehead and taking my hands in his.

"It's a long story." I emitted a fake laugh, stepping aside so that he, and Jess of course, could come in.

"We have time," he replied, checking his watch. I sat on my floor in the living room near the electric fire that I had turned on at full heat, turning to face them.

"Let's start with Clayton Devis, I guess," I said, leaning my head on my knees wearily. They glanced at each other and then back at me.

"Who?" Jess finally asked, looking confused.

"Clayton," I repeated, gesturing in the shape of a guy. "Big jock asshole in our grade? Dating Sterling? Luke punched him the other day?"

"Riley, you're talking about Matt Danison," Luke frowned. I studied their faces in surprise.

"You don't remember Clayton?"

"I don't think there's ever been a Clayton at our school, Rye," Jess said, feeling my forehead carefully, avoiding the bruise. "Maybe she has a concussion," she muttered over her shoulder to Luke.

Chapter Nine

I do not!" I snapped, knocking her hand away. "I have proof that Clayton existed!" I ran up to my room, grabbing the bone out of my jacket and hurrying back downstairs. "Here," I said, shoving it at Luke first.

"Is that a bone?" Jess gagged, leaning away. I waved it at Luke again, and he took it gingerly, pinching it in between his thumb and finger. Then he keeled over.

"Luke!" I gasped, slapping his face gently until he woke up groggily.

"I can't believe I forgot Clayton," he said, sitting up.

"You remember?" I said, taking the finger back from him and examining it. Maybe the goblins had put a spell on it?

"Clayton wasn't a real person, guys," Jess said, warily moving away from us. I offered her the bone but she cringed away in disgust.

"Catch," I said, throwing it into her lap. She passed out too, taking a full five minutes to wake up.

"Clayton," she said, forehead wrinkling as the memories came rushing back.

"Wait," Luke said, turning to me, "what about Clayton?"

I told them the entire story, starting with my mom slapping me and ending with big boy and his goblin friends.

"Oh, sweetie," Jess said, wrapping her arms around me, "why is your life so hard?"

"Oh, the hard life of a privileged white girl," I said and laughed thickly, swallowing my tears. I can't believe I even had any tears left after my shower.

"Doesn't mean your life is easy," Luke murmured in my ear, joining in the group hug.

"So what are we going to do?" Jess asked when we had broken apart.

"We have to stop them before they kill anyone else and make us forget about it, right?" Luke answered, both of them looking at me for instructions.

"We should research them first," I decided, "just so we know what we're fighting and how to kill them. I mean, why didn't you guys remember Clayton until you touched the bone? And why and how did the goblins make you forget?"

"Good idea." Jess nodded in approval. "Where do you want to start?"

"The library?" I suggested.

"Let's go," Luke agreed, taking my hand and not letting go until we reached the library.

When we got there, they were already closing but Luke bribed the main librarian to let us stay, promising that we would put everything back correctly and that we needed to do research for a last minute project. She agreed, after he gave her his number and promised to pay for anything that wasn't in perfect condition by tomorrow morning, we just had to be out by one in the morning and lock the doors after us. "Want to start with myths or see what they have on goblins?" Luke asked after we had promised for a fifth time that everything would be fine and she had left.

"Let's start with myths," I replied, walking toward a computer and typing in as many keywords as I could think of until I hit the jackpot. *"Kallikantzaroi, Demons of the Night"* I read, the cover picture looking exactly like the creatures in the woods. "It's in the fiction section." We tracked it down, pulling it off the shelf and opening the cover. A cloud of dust greeted us, making me cough and choke. They read over my shoulder while I skimmed the first couple of pages. "This is definitely them," I said, pointing to a section claiming that kallikantzaroi could mimic the voices of loved ones. "The ones in the woods used Sterling's voice to control Clayton. And they came up from the dirt," I added, tracing a line claiming that the ancient Greeks thought that the Special K came from the underworld (from now on we will call the kallikantzaroi as Special K because honestly I'm giving myself concussions trying to pronounce that word over and over).

"This says that they can only come up from the underworld on Christmas." Jess frowned, flipping the page. "How can they appear in the forest?"

"How am I supposed to know?" I asked, turning the page again, "I only started learning about these too. You can go ask them if you want." The rest of the book was the writer rambling on about how they can only count to two, because the word three would kill them. I skipped to the very last chapter on how to protect yourself.

"Can you recount every detail of what they were and looked like and did?" Luke queried, pulling up a chair next to me. I recited the story for them again, sparing no details, even telling them about the noises until Jess swayed on her feet, turning pale.

"Maybe we should research their king," Luke proposed, "Or the forest."

"How would we even find their king?" Jess said hopelessly.

"With a computer," I said, rolling my eyes at her. I walked back to the reference desk, pulling up Google. *King of Goblins* I typed, hitting enter and groaning at the results. "These are all fictional characters," I complained, scrolling through them.

"Maybe he's a god, not a king," Luke said, glancing up from his book. I deleted my search and typed in *God of Goblins* instead.

"This is all stuff for dungeons and dragons," I said. "What else have you got?"

"Try *God of Evil*," Jess said. I tried it, and thousands of results popped up.

"This is him," I cried when I saw the picture provided. "His name is Apollyon and he's the angel of the bottomless pit. He came up from a crack in the earth!"

"We know," Luke smirked, "you've told us twice."

"Well, excuse me for being thorough," I grimaced at him, sticking out my tongue.

"How are we going to fight a god?" Jess wondered, burying her head in her arms in desperation.

"He's not a real god, relax," I said. "He's just an angel that happens to monopolize an area that no one really wants, so he's basically a god but his powers can't be that strong or he wouldn't need an army of Special K to get humans for him to feed on. And he would have been able to sense me, right?"

"That's true," Luke agreed. "He has to be a pretty lame god. So we take down his army and then we kill him."

"Why do we have to do any of this?" I asked, hating how hysterical I sounded. "We've never killed anything before, guys. I should probably ask my mom before I try to kill stuff."

"Are you saying you don't think we can kill stuff?" Luke frowned at me, and added, "because it can't be that hard."

"It has to be hard enough!" I cried. "We have no training, no special skills and no weapons either. I have a pocket knife, which I don't think is enough to take down an army of Special K."

"So we train." He shrugged. "We have three weeks."

"And I suppose you want a training montage with inspirational music too, right?" I said, shaking my head in exasperation. "That's not how this works!"

"So we go to your parents and if they don't remember Clayton and don't believe us then we go to the gun range tomorrow after school and we learn, Riley. We can't just let creatures of the underworld kill our townspeople and then erase our memories."

"Where are you going to even get three guns?" Jess inquired, joining our conversation.

"Being rich and white can get you anything in this country my friends," he replied, winking.

"Fine," I surrendered, throwing up my hands in defeat, "but we go to our parents first, is that clear?"

"Crystal." He beamed, and I shook my head. This was going to be a long month.

We gave up on the research around midnight, locking up and trekking home. Luke and Jess refused to let me walk home by myself, but I was worried about them too so they ended up calling Mrs. Moore to drive them home. I let myself into the house, shrieking in surprise when I saw my mom sitting on the stairs. "Why are you sitting in the dark?" I hissed at her. She got up in one fluid motion, running over to hug me.

"I was so worried about you." She sniffed, pulling me close.

"Are you okay?" I frowned, drawing back.

"I'm sorry I didn't take your side," she said, cupping my face in her hands. "And I'm sorry I hit you. I was so afraid that you had gone into the woods when we couldn't find you."

"You know about it, don't you," I said, pushing her away and standing back. "Why else would you be worried about the woods? It's not like I was that far away."

"Know about what?" she said innocently.

"Special K and big boy!" I said loudly. She shushed me gently and a look of real confusion crossed her face.

"I really have no idea what you're talking about." She frowned.

"The Kallikantzaroi and whoever controls them." I motioned to the back window where the woods were shining in the moonlight. Her eyes widened in fear, and she pulled me into another hug.

"Oh, Riley," she muttered into my hair, "you were in the woods last night. You know you're not supposed to be there after sunset." I nodded, swiping at my eyes before they could drip on her. "Who did they get this time?" she asked sadly.

"Clayton," I said. "How?"

"Do I know about them?" she finished. "They come every year, and it's the mayor's job to control them. That's why the curse was made. These princes, they were born for it, Riley. Let them handle it." All I could do was walk past her, up the stairs to my room where I locked my door and collapsed on my bed in a deep sleep before I had to deal with any more shocking revelations for today.

That morning, my mom was back to normal. She handed me an apple on my way out of the house, (Alex still hadn't made an appearance at the table I noticed. I bet he was hiding in his room out of vainness, not wanting anyone to see his battle scars) and gave me an unfeeling peck on the cheek. I took my time going to school, then sat at my locker until Luke showed up and we went to our first period class together. Nothing seemed different or out of place; there was no mourning the loss of a classmate, so whatever the Special K army had done was working. The only real difference was the brunette boy on Sterling's arm, instead of the ever-present Clayton. She seemed unaffected, and I felt a wave of jealousy for all the ignorance that my peers had been blessed with.

"So did you talk to your mom?" Luke asked in English class when the teacher turned away to pull up a PowerPoint on her computer. I nodded, scribbling him a note detailing the conversation between my mom and me very early this morning. "And they think that Alex is the best person to control these creatures?" he hissed, so incredulous that his eyebrows disappeared into his hair.

"I guess," I said and shrugged. "I think they care more about his royal blood than anything else."

"He's royal?" Luke smirked. "Why do I doubt that?"

"He's like third cousins to the second cousin of the distant uncle of the first cousin of the Belgium Royal Family," I said. "It was the best that they could do in a pinch. No one with actual royal blood is going to want to come rule our crappy little town, right?"

"I would want to rule this crappy little town," Luke said, lifting a shoulder. "Either that or run far, far away to a different continent."

"Can I come with?" I asked jokingly. "No, I can't!" I objected when he nodded fervently. "You know I have to stay here and watch Alex screw up the town. It's part of the deal with the curse, you of all people should know that."

"We could still just change your name," he offered grinning.

"Let's try and live through the goblin-pocolypse and go from there," I replied, closing my mouth with a click when my teacher turned to glare at me.

"Goblin-pocalypse," Luke mused, tapping his chin. "I like that. We should make merchandise that says 'I survived the goblin-pocalypse' and sell it to the people who want to tell their grandchildren about us."

"Not a bad idea," I agreed.

"I think we should still go to the gun range," Luke decided after school.

"But I talked to my mom," I protested.

"And she thinks that Alex is going to help us," he pointed out. "So we should probably figure out how to defend ourselves so that we might actually survive the goblin-pocalypse and sell t-shirts."

"It's true," Jess agreed. "And you said you didn't want a prince protecting you."

"Fine," I said, biting my lip. I was against guns, but if they were to fight goblins then I figured that seemed like an exception.

I was surprisingly good at shooting the gun. Luke had hired us an instructor who taught us how to stand and where to point and everything, and then let us go. We got earplugs and targets and were told that we could shoot until we ran out of rounds. Jess screamed every time she pulled the trigger, which made everything more interesting of course, and Luke flinched, hitting the walls more than the target. My hand wasn't steady at first, and I kept hitting the target in the leg, but the more comfortable I got with the kick back the closer I got to the center. "Damn," Luke said when he saw how I was doing.

"Thanks," I grinned, putting a neat hole through the target's mouth.

"I really can't do this, guys," Jess said, shuddering and placing the gun carefully on the counter.

"It's okay." Luke grinned. "Riley will protect you."

"True." I nodded, shooting another bullet straight through the target's chest.

We had to buy Jess hot chocolate to console her after the gun range. I couldn't tell if she was upset because of the violence she had used against the paper cutout of a body or because she was bad at violence, and I decided not to ask. We hit the library afterwards, doing more research on how to kill Special K armies, but we couldn't find anything. Surprisingly, the world didn't stop moving through all of this so we still had homework to do. It was so late by the time that we had finished our homework that we just went home after. We didn't bring up the curse again until the following week; once there was a reason behind the curse, the guilt was overpowering to try and stop it. By the time we actually revisited the subject, I only had two weeks left.

This is an awkward transition to a week later when there was a week until Christmas, meaning six days until my birthday, when the Special K could actually come up from the underground which they were apparently already doing (I hope that long run-on sentence gave you a headache). We were all so stressed out with the Special K and the lamest god ever that we had decided to go Christmas shopping instead of the endless research we had thrown ourselves into. I had already bought my dad a spatula, Alex a pair of socks and my mom a bracelet. I was hoping the shininess would distract her from the fact that I hadn't slept at home in three days.

I had been sleeping at Jess's to avoid Alex who in the span of a week, (which was barely enough to fade the bruise on his chin) had decided that he needed to ambush me any time I was home and ask personal questions about my life so that he could get to know me in the second creepiest way ever. He had already gotten to know my fist in the first creepiest way. Jess and Luke had actually tried with their gifts, over-thinking all of them to the point where I wanted to scream. I escaped, ending up at the food court with a pretzel where I was cornered by Sterling and replacement Clayton. "Don't you know how many calories are in that?" she sneered, wrinkling her nose haughtily.

"Well, the amount I care is congruent with the amount of brain cells you have left," I smiled, making a zero with my pointer finger and thumb. Wannabe Clayton coughed to hide his snort, and I winked at him.

"You're not that great," she yelled after me when I started to walk away.

"Yes, I am," I called back, purposefully swinging my hips until I could feel every eye on me. Then I turned around, blowing her a kiss and noting with satisfaction how replacement Clayton was watching me with an open mouth. "Your boyfriend's drooling," I added, smirking when she elbowed him in the ribs, and walking back to where I had left Luke and Jess. They were still arguing about the sentimental value of a tie clip.

As Christmas drew closer, our stress levels grew in a direct relationship, until the point where Jess burst into tears over the "five minutes until closing" announcement at the library one night. "It's going to be okay," I said, rubbing her back and shooting an exasperated look over her shoulder to Luke.

"No, it's not," she blubbered. The librarian came over to see if we were okay, and I waved her away with a shrug.

"PMS," I mouthed to her, and she nodded, satisfied. We walked Jess home after that. She was too tired to protest, and she knew that she wasn't going to be that much help. Our daily visits to the gun range weren't helping either. Luke had stopped flinching and I had hit the target's chest more times than not but Jess was still too squeamish about shooting anyone even if they were made out of paper. Luke and I wandered back to my house in silence, holding hands after dropping her off, until he suddenly stopped. I didn't notice until my arm was yanked back and I had to turn around so it wouldn't come out its socket. He let go of my hand and it dropped to my side. "What?" I asked, studying his face.

"I love you," he said quietly. I froze in shock.

"What?"

"I love you," he repeated, louder this time. I sat down in the middle of the sidewalk, mind spinning. He sat down across from me. "I love you," he said again, lifting my chin so that I had to look at him.

"Thanks," I said, standing back up and backing away from him. I turned back to the direction of my house and started to walk faster.

"Hey," he said, catching up to me and grabbing my arm. "You don't have to love me back and you can be freaked out all you want but there are goblin monsters attacking in a week and you're marrying someone else so I'm going to damn well say how I feel before the world ends or you're stuck as a happy housewife," he finished, looking at me expectantly.

"We've only been dating for two weeks," I said, my voice breaking. "You can't love me that quickly, this isn't a *Disney* movie, Luke. You're just complicating things that were already plenty complicated to begin with and it's not fair."

"Since when does the world care about fair," Luke said, his hands in the air. "Life isn't fair. Just look at the obscene amount of money everyone in this town has. And none of them deserve it. And you're being married off to a guy, whose nose you broke, because of little evil goblins. That's not fair. You didn't ask for little goblin creatures to live behind your house, but they do. And I didn't ask to meet you freshmen year but I'm glad I did."

"It's only been two weeks," I reiterated, shaking my head. "You don't fall in love with someone over the span of two weeks. That's not how it works."

"I didn't fall in love with you today, Riley, or two weeks ago, or a month ago, or a year ago. I fell in love with you in sophomore year, and I was too much of a coward to do anything until now. And how does it work, Rye? Please." He opened his arms widely, gesturing around us. "Enlighten me in the way of love, your highness." He gave me a mocking bow.

"I don't know," I shouted, "but this isn't it."

"I don't care what you say," he yelled, anger crossing his face, "I love you, Riley Owens and you can do whatever the fuck you want with that information, but don't patronize me or tell me that this isn't real because you don't know me." I recoiled, stung.

"Maybe I don't know you," I snapped, tears spilling down my face.

"No, hey, Rye," he said, cupping my chin gently. I pulled back and he sighed. "You know that's not what I meant."

"I know what you meant," I said, dangerously quiet. "Maybe I don't know you Luke and that's fine with me because this was doomed from the beginning and you know it."

"You're wrong," he said, coldly strong. "We're not doomed. We can get through this Riley."

"How?" I asked, pushing his shoulder, refusing to calm down. "How is shooting things going to fix this mess, Luke? Because I don't remember how to shoot a curse. How do you shoot a curse, Luke?" His eyes glittered darkly at my words, an angry twist to his mouth. Then he grabbed me by the waist and pulled me against him, leaning down until his lips almost reached mine. He paused, with a centimeter in between us and I realized that he was asking for permission. I groaned, knowing that I would regret it if I kissed him; it would make everything so much more complicated. But I did it anyway. He held me closer to his chest as his lips gently separated mine, and I wrapped my arms around his neck, inhaling the smell of him (but not in a creepy way I swear). I shivered against the cold and he drew away, but not far.

"Stay at my house," he murmured, nose touching mine lightly. I nodded hesitatingly, and he led me back in the direction we had gone.

His mom greeted us at the door, but didn't ask questions when he dragged me up the stairs towards his room, except to yell, "Be safe! No unplanned pregnancies in this house!" She really was the best. He threw himself down on his bed, pulling me down on top of him. I kissed him again, and his hand slid under my shirt, fumbling with my bra. I shook my head, still covering his lips with mine, and I felt him smile, retracting his hand. He didn't push it, and after a (very fun) twenty minutes, we came up for air, and I rolled down next to him. He clapped his hands and the lights turned off (because that's how rich people do it) and wrapped his arms around me. I rested my head on his chest, and he kissed the top of it, drifting off to sleep way before I even shut my eyes.

When I woke up Luke had his arms around me and I was cradled into his chest. The sun was rising, so I climbed over him carefully and tiptoed downstairs. Mrs. Moore was sitting at the table in the kitchen drinking out of a mug. "Want coffee?" she asked, looking up from the newspaper she was reading.

"Sure," I said, and she handed me a plate of waffles and a cup of coffee. "Thanks!"

"I called your mom, and the school already," she replied with a knowing smile.

"Thanks," I repeated, relieved. I didn't want to show up to school in the same clothes as before. Oh wait, I always wear the same clothes (get it? It's because I have a uniform! I crack myself up).

"So, three more days until winter break, huh?" she said, breaking the awkward silence that I had created while stuffing waffles in my mouth. I cleared my throat, swallowing hurriedly. "What are you going to do with all that free time?"

"Run from goblins, how about you?" I answered without thinking.

"Sounds like fun," she said with a nod, going back to her newspaper. "I, for one, am going to be pouring a border of salt around my house."

"Does that work?" I said, like I was asking if she would pass the sugar.

"Keeps them out."

I arched an eyebrow at her doubtfully, taking another bite of waffles. I wasn't sure I wanted to know how she knew that much about small demon goblin things. As if she had read my mind, she stood up, walking upstairs and returning with a book. *101 Spells for Every Witch's Need*, the title said. On the cover was a crystal ball surrounded by trees that looked like they were breathing out mist. "You're kidding," I said, shaking my head at her, fighting back a smile.

"Don't judge me for what I buy on Amazon in the middle of the night," she said, frowning at me and taking it back. She flipped to a page that was folded down at the corner, handing it to me to see.

"How to protect your home from negative energy," I read aloud, trying to repress an eye roll so aggressive that it threatened to burst the blood vessels in my head. I skimmed the page, looking back up at her when I had gotten halfway down. "This says to burn sage bundles," I said, wondering what the author did with their day on the daily basis. I imagined a lot of smoking was involved. She took the book back, frowning slightly at me.

"Have you ever spilled salt and been told to throw some over your shoulder?" she recited, looking back up for dramatic emphasis before continuing. "That's because in some cultures it is believed that the devil is waiting for you, and the salt will blind him, keeping him distracted. There is some truth in this, however. Since salt is used for curing and preserving food, it is believed to be blessed with immortality and purity. Evil spirits will be repelled from salt because of this. It will preserve the good energy in your home, keeping the devil, and his friends away."

"Are we actually basing the safety of an entire town on a book that was probably written in a peyote fueled haze?" I said, rubbing my forehead with my hand to get rid of the pressure building behind my temples.

"It's more than anything else I could find," she said, suddenly looking as tired as I felt. I winced with guilt, attempting a smile.

"I'm sorry, you're right. At least we have that to go off of. Thank you so much for finding that," I said, reaching across the table and squeezing her hand. We went back to eating waffles in comfortable silence, the book cover down between us, with the author's picture smiling innocently to the ceiling.

Luke woke up twenty minutes later, plodding down the stairs sleepily.

"Hey," he said, kissing his mom on the cheek and grabbing waffles off the stove. "Hey," he repeated, leaning down to kiss me on the lips.

"Gross," his mom commented, looking over the top of the paper at us and wrinkling her nose.

"Thanks, Mrs. Moore." I grinned, pulling away from him. He sat down next to me and glared at his mom, who blew him a distracted kiss. I ate slowly, staring blankly at the clock. Finally, Mr. Moore, who had joined us and stolen the newspaper from his wife with a coercive kiss that made me and Luke cringe, checked his watch.

"Why don't you bring Riley home, Lucas?" he suggested, and Luke caught my eye with a silent question.

"Okay." I nodded, standing up and putting my dish in the sink. We were quiet on the way home, but a good quiet, not "about to drop a bombshell about love" quiet. He kissed me gently at my front steps, and when I got inside I leaned against the door breathlessly.

"Where were you?" Alex asked, appearing with his arms crossed.

"Haven't seen you in a while," I said cheerfully, raising my eyebrows. "If I had known that punching you would have that effect I would have done it sooner." He backed away after I said that, but continued to follow me to the kitchen as I grabbed a bottle of water out of the fridge. The right side of his face still had a slight purpling blush, but besides that it was like my knuckles never touched him.

"Where were you?" he repeated, leaning against the wall and blocking my path.

"My boyfriend's house." I smirked, moving to the left to squeeze past him. He slapped me hard across the face, and I snapped backwards as he breathed heavily.

"Whore," he said as I was reeling.

"Why is everyone hitting me lately?" I cried, holding my face. He tilted closer into my face.

"You're mine," he hissed. "Remember that." I responded with a calm smile despite my throbbing cheek. "What?" he frowned, taking an unnerved step back.

"You hit me," I said, matching his step.

"And?"

"You're fair game," I said sweetly, bringing my arm around in a right hook, making a matching bruise on his left cheekbone. "I'm no one's," I said, pushing him out of the way as he crumpled. "People *don't* belong to people."

My mom found me in my room while I was holding the water bottle to my face and my knuckles to keep the swelling down. "Did he start it?" She sighed, taking in my battered appearance. I nodded in surprise. "That's what I thought. He wouldn't tell me what happened." She examined my face tiredly. "I'm sorry," she added when she finally started to leave. "I know you didn't ask for this." Ten minutes later, she came back in. "Have you seen your grandma?" she asked, a baffled expression on her face that was downright adorable. I shrugged and shook my head, and she left again. I spent the rest of the day lying on my bed staring at the ceiling until my mom called me for dinner. I noted with satisfaction that Alex was nowhere to be found, having locked himself in his room again.

Waking up for school the next day was easier because of my day off. Everyone at school was in Christmas mode, since we got out for Christmas break in three days. Unfortunately, that meant that the teachers were in "missing a week of learning" mindset, and I had test after test that I had either forgotten about or forgotten to study for. My brain was in full panic setting during my slog through the history test on India, and refused to process anything by my chemistry test at the end of the day. I ran down the multiple choice with complete haphazardness, making a pattern. The door creaked open, causing the entire class to look up for a much needed break. Sterling was standing awkwardly in the front of the class. It made me feel better to see her out of her element, but unfortunately, she caught my smile and shot me a sneer, making my class focus their attention on me. "How can I help you?" my teacher asked, getting up and walking to the front of the room. Sterling flashed her a light smile, handing her an envelope.

"I have something for Riley Owens," she chirped.

"She can have it after she's done with her test," my teacher said, glaring at me and then back at Sterling, as if accusing us of cheating.

"Perfect," Sterling said, relaxing my teacher's suspicious face. She backed out slowly, giving me a cheerful wave, and blowing me a kiss. I stared at the envelope in my teacher's hand, wondering what Sterling had in store for me. I wasn't disappointed. I handed in my test, taking the envelope in return and going back to my seat in the back of the room, then waited for Luke to give the teacher his test before sliding my finger under the flap of it and taking the sheet of paper out of it. *Missing something?* was scribbled across it in boldly angry letters.

"Not that I know of," I muttered, Luke giving me a sideways look. I shrugged at him and crumpled it up, throwing it out on my way out of the class. Luke took the envelope out of my hand while we were walking towards the lockers, and inspected the inside.

"This has instructions in it," he announced, ripping the seams of the envelope and flattening it into a sheet of paper.

"Read them," I said, glancing up at him and then back at my open locker.

"Saturday, eight o'clock at night, room 204," he said, showing me the words in the cramped handwriting that I recognized as Sterling's.

"Why does she want to see me on the day before my birthday?" I frowned, taking the envelope from him.

"Maybe she wants to throw you a surprise party," Luke suggested hopefully.

"Oh, optimism." I laughed and added, "I've missed that. I'm assuming whatever it is, she wants to talk about whatever I'm 'missing'."

"Fine, use logic," he grumbled.

"With what?" Jess asked, joining us.

"I think we need to, like, get Bluetooth and listen to all of our conversations with each other because explaining things to whichever one isn't there is exhausting," I said with a groan, launching into a rerun of my conversation with Luke.

Chapter Ten

Saturday was a mess. My mom woke me up at six in the morning, with a hysterical rush of words centering on my absent grandma. "You still haven't found her?" I grumbled into my pillow.

"No," she cried, throwing up her hands. "She promised that she would help me with your party!"

"We're having a party?" I muttered. "For what, the fact that I can legally vote?" She held up here hands in surrender again.

"You're impossible in the morning, you know that right?"

"Yep," I replied, rolling over and going back to sleep. The second time I was woken up was by the doorbell ringing at seven. After that, distant relatives wandered in and out of my room, dropping kisses on my forehead and then leaving. There was a small crowd of people in the living room when I decided that this was no condition to sleep well under. They cheered when I descended the stairs and at least ten of them offered me breakfast. I waved them all off, squeezing past them into the kitchen. My mom had her most practiced smile on, handing out plates of scrambled eggs to the people milling around the room. "They're like ants," I mumbled through a mouthful of eggs when we were finally alone.

"They're not that bad," she said through a gritted grin, giving breakfast to my second cousin twice removed, who pecked me on the cheek and sashayed away.

"I'm going to Luke's," I announced, taking a quick sip of juice and putting my dish in the sink. She shot me a pleading look, but I waved and ran through my door. When I was down the block, I relaxed. I took my time getting to Luke's. He opened the door the second I took my finger off the doorbell and let me in.

"You're here early," he said as he yawned. "My parents are still sleeping."

"Sorry," I said, letting him take my coat. "My family invaded my house. There are at least fifty people and I don't know a single one of them. I had to get out of there before they started telling me how tall I was and how much I've grown up since they saw me last."

"I wasn't complaining that you're here," he grinned, leaning down to kiss me. "Want breakfast?"

"No, thanks," I said, flopping down on his couch. "My mom made an assembly line making too many scrambled eggs."

"Sounds like fun," he said, nodding as he sat down next to me. He saw me eyeing his shelf. "Want to watch a movie then?"

"Sure," I said, pulling *Mulan* off the stack next to the TV.

"I thought you said no more Disney," he said, checking out my choice.

"She's the only good Disney princess," I said, popping the movie into the machine and settling down next to him. His parents joined us halfway through the movie, laughing along with the talking dragon. After *Mulan* was done, I found out that they owned *Mulan II*, which I made them watch of course. And by the end of that movie, we were all in the mood for a serious *Disney* marathon, and by the time we were done it was already five o'clock. "I should go." I sighed, standing up and stretching. I gave Mrs. Moore a hug, and she refused to let go long after I had. She pulled back and looked me in the eyes.

"You don't need a prince to save you," she said, holding my face firmly. I saw the tears sparkling in her eyes, making my bottom lip tremble horribly.

"I know," I said, laughing, my voice breaking.

"We'll see you when you wake up," Mr. Moore said, giving me a tighter hug than his wife had. I nodded, biting my traitorous lip.

"I think I'm going to stay at Riley's tonight," he told his parents when we were finally out of the door. They exchanged wise looks and gave him a thumbs-up while closing the door. I could have sworn I saw Mrs. Moore mouth "condoms" at him before they were shut away.

My family attacked us with questions when we walked into my house holding hands. "Is he your boyfriend?" one scandalized aunt asked, and when I assented, the younger generation broke into appreciative applause and my older relatives sniffed disapprovingly. I suffered through more bombarding at dinner, which Luke took the brunt of politely. Then we were forced into a family game of trivial pursuit, which I purposefully lost in order to be excused. By seven thirty, everyone was so sick of each other that we all went to separate rooms of the house and said goodnight. I sat on my bed, Luke sitting below me on the floor.

"What do you want to do?" he asked, and I shrugged.

"Whatever you want to do."

He checked his watch and sighed. "We have about a half an hour before the meeting time. Can we make it through the front door?" I got up, sticking my head into the hallway and listening. I could still hear the distant chatter of people in the living room. I closed my door again, shaking my head. "Does your secret passage lead to any outside areas?"

"My parents were too afraid I would sneak out and never come back after I found out about the curse," I admitted.

"Climbing out the window it is then," he said, taking me into his lap. He leaned against my wall, arms wrapped around my stomach.

"Sounds good," I agreed, twisting around so I could look at him. "I know you want to come with me, but don't come into the room with me, please."

"What?" he exclaimed, almost pitching me off his legs. "Sorry," he apologized, centering me again.

"If it's Sterling, then it will probably be something socially humiliating. And since I have a chance of sleeping for a hundred years, and you don't you're not coming with me. Plus, collectively we could greatly damage Jess's 'cool' status, but with only one of us then she can always claim that she doesn't know me," I reasoned.

"Fine," he consented, kissing the hollow of my neck, before trailing his lips all the way up to my ear, "but I don't like it."

"Who cares if you like it," I teased.

All too soon, it was time to go. Luke climbed down first, carefully testing each branch. I followed, swinging from branch to branch like a monkey. He helped me down at the bottom and we exchanged glances before breaking into a run. We ran down my driveway, and half a block until I slowed to a trot, trying to catch my breath.

"You're really out of breath," he said and laughed, circling back to where I was. "I'm not sure that one hundred years of sleep is really going to help that."

"Shut up," I gasped, doubling over. Maybe I should have jogged more in preparation of this. We dragged our feet to the school, pulling at the doors until we found the one that Sterling had unlocked for us. The entire school was dark, and we had to feel our way inside. I made Luke wait in the entrance while I crept upstairs to my chemistry classroom. The light was on, and I could hear voices from inside, all of them eerily familiar, but not in a classmate kind of way. I knocked quietly, and the lights flickered out leaving the hallway pitch black again. I heard the creak of the door, but I couldn't even see the hands in front of my face. Unfortunately, whoever hit me over the head, knocking me out, had probably been relying on that fact.

I woke up with ropes biting into my wrists and ankles and a blindfold on. I tensed, feeling cold metal pressed against my arms and legs, and plastic against my back. Out of all the things I could have been tied to, it was one of the damn school chairs. Wasn't it bad enough that I had been sitting on them for thirteen years of my life? (Yes, this was in fact my first reaction to being bound and gagged in a foreign situation). My head was throbbing in the back where I had been hit and every time I tried to lift my head, the pain of it resisted in earnest. I pulled experimentally at the ropes, but nothing happened. It was very anticlimactic; I was hoping that the bindings would just fall away like they did for people in the movies. I took a deep breath to calm my shaking knees and tried to open my eyes again. The blindfold was so tight against my head that I could only open them halfway before my eyelashes were in the way.

I tried to move my upper body and found that only my wrists were tied; the rest of my body was free, save for my ankles. I bent my head to my thighs, ignoring the sharp pain of having my arms twisting in a weird angle behind me, grabbing where the blindfold arched over my nose between my knees. I pulled my head back, and to my surprise the blindfold gave way. I sat back up, blinking my eyes open slowly. I was in my chemistry classroom, the moon shining through the window and lighting a slow path. I tilted my neck to get the kinks out and looked around. I was alone. I took in my tied wrists and ankles and trying not to taste whatever they had shoved in my mouth. I tried to spit it out, but something else was tied around the lower half of my face, sealing in what I discovered was a sock, after I unfortunately moved my tongue. I froze when I heard footsteps in the hallway, and closed my eyes again.

"She's still not up," I heard someone say exasperatedly to someone else. I knew that voice, but I couldn't quite put my finger on it. Ond of them turned the light on, the red glow flooding through my eyelids making my temples ache.

"They don't call her sleeping beauty for nothing," another voice replied with a cackle. I knew that voice anywhere; Sterling has a very distinct laugh, known for piercing the eardrums of even the strongest men. (These two people will henceforth be known as Dumb and Dumber for your future reference; Sterling is definitely dumber, but it's a tossup).

"She is beautiful," Dumb agreed, and a hand reached down to stroke my cheek. I resisted the urge to flinch at the touch, focusing on pretending to be asleep. My breaths were choppy and short, but Dumb and Dumber didn't notice.

"You can have her after we're done, brother dearest," Dumber said in a bored tone. Of course, Sterling always spoke in a bored tone so that might just have been her voice.

"Well, after we're done with her then I won't want her, will I," Dumb argued grumpily. I definitely knew that voice, but from where? Dumber paused before answering.

"We still have…" I assumed she checked the time, but I actually have no idea because my eyes were closed. The problem with first-person narration. …"twenty minutes before midnight, if you want to have her now," she suggested.

"Not a bad idea, sis," Dumb agreed. I stiffened at their words, hoping that they hadn't noticed my movement. I felt what I assumed were Dumb's fingers, since as far as I knew Sterling wasn't into girls, moving down and then back up my face, and then tilting my cheek. His fingers fumbled at the cloth holding the sock in place, pulling it over my

87

head when it was loose enough. I whimpered quietly when the gag brought some of my hair with it, still tied into the knot, and he paused. I held a lungful of air until my heart stopped racing, then let it out, in slow, easy breaths. Satisfied that I was asleep, he pried my mouth open, tugging out the sock, and carefully cleaning the spit that had come with it off of my chin. He pressed his lips to mine, and a sudden spark down my spine announced who it was. I bit down hard, opening my eyes and slamming my already pained head into Alex's, who stepped back, swearing.

"Look," Sterling said, stepping closer. "A kiss from your true love *did* wake you up."

"He's not my true love," I snapped, spitting on the floor next to her feet. Not to be aggressive or anything; I just needed to get the sock taste out of my taste buds. Dumb's mouth was bleeding at the corner, a product of my teeth. I smiled proudly as he stepped forward, then decided better of it and retreated to the corner. "So, brother and sister," I said, pretending to mull it over. "Are you twins? Because from what I can tell, you guys share one brain cell that's about to die from loneliness." I punctuated my sentence with a confident smirk; the effect was ruined by my bottom lip trembling with nerves of what they were going to do to me.

"Just brother and sister," she answered chirpily, her peppiness concerning me immediately. "We're a big happy family. Want to meet our third member?"

"Not particularly," I replied. "I think you two are ugly enough. My eyes might not survive another Sterling Alex."

"That's too bad, because she *really* wants to meet you," Dumber said, her voice thick with fake concern. She nodded towards the door, which swung open.

"My mom's looking for you, by the way," I said to my grandma who was hobbling through the doorway. I mirrored my mom's perfect stillness, refusing to let them see me squirm. I was rewarded by the exchange of surprised glances that they gave each other. "You were supposed to help with my birthday party," I added, pouting so they couldn't see the quiver in my chin.

"You don't even want to know why she's working with us?"

Dumber finally burst out, after another confused silence.

"Not really." I shrugged (or as well as I could move my shoulders with my wrists tied), "but I have the feeling that you want to tell me so go ahead." I tilted my head attentively, and added, "I'm all ears."

"Well first, she's not your real grandma," Sterling started, walking slowly across the room in what I perceived as a mockingly pensive pace.

"Yes, I know," I interrupted, rolling my eyes. "She's my step-grandma."

"Oh," Dumber said, slightly rattled. She rebounded on her back foot, continuing her pacing. "Well, she's our real Grandma." An unwilling gasp expanded my lungs, and Dumber smiled, satisfied.

"Actually," I said, really thinking about it, "I knew there was no way that someone as cool as her was in my family without having an ulterior motive. I doubt she would have survived if she didn't need to carry out a nefarious plot."

"It's not that nefarious," my grandma said, taking a step closer to me and holding out her hand.

"I wouldn't do that if I were you," Dumb warned from the corner, still trying to stop his bleeding. I accentuated his sentence by snapping my teeth at her outstretched fingers. She withdrew them hurriedly, shaking her head disapprovingly at me.

"It's almost time," Sterling announced, after what I estimated to be about five minutes. She looked me up and down, an unnerving grin on her lips. I held her gaze coldly, yanking desperately on my bindings. I felt the rope cutting into my veins and a trickle of blood ran down and dripped off my pinky.

"Want to get her ready?" Dumb asked.

"We can do that afterwards," Dumber replied, still sizing me up. "I don't trust her without the ropes on." Dumb rubbed his face reminiscently and nodded.

"Smart," he agreed. They sat in a comfortable silence, while I shook like a leaf, not even bothering to hide it. I was on the verge of tears in the still air, nothing but the aggravating tick of the clock to keep me company. An annoying burst of sound made me jump, the ropes scraping roughly at my legs. Sterling reached into her back pocket, shutting the alarm on her phone off. I guessed it was midnight. Happy birthday to me.

"You want to do the honors?" Sterling asked Alex, who nodded. They sounded like they were talking about taking the last cookie. She reached into a bag behind her, pulling out a knife unceremoniously and handed it to him. He reached into his back pocket, extracting a green vial, which he uncorked with his teeth carefully and let a drop slide down the opening and onto the tip of the knife. I gritted my teeth when a tear slid down my cheek, wiping it on my shoulder before they noticed. I held my head up straight, looking Alex dead in the eye when he walked over to me.

"Hold your breath," he snarled with a smirk, cutting one of my arms loose, and before I could react, plunging the tip of the blade into my vein. The last thing I felt before everything went black was the warm flow of blood down my arm, the ground shaking beneath us. I struggled to keep my eyes open as Alex released me from my chair, lying me down on top of a pillow, before all three of them disappeared and rose vines pushed their way out of the ground to wrap me in a prison of thorns.

Chapter Eleven

Luke

I was sitting in the front hall of our school when everything went black. I could feel the impact as something collided with my head, and the last thing I could feel before I succumbed to darkness was the thud of my ear against the wooden bench. When I woke up I could feel the rattling of windows as an earthquake started. I pushed myself off of the bench, breaking into a sprint. I took the stairs two at a time, skidding into the hallway where Riley should have been.

Rose vines were wrapping their way around the doorways, exploding the windows and cracking the doors. I narrowly avoided the shards of glass, pushing my way through the thorns towards the quickly disappearing door. I swore as a vine scratched my face and another one pierced my hand. I stared desperately at the chemistry room, the roses throwing me backward with surprising force.

"I'll be back," I muttered to her, before turning around and running back the way I had come. I turned to look back at the school, vines bursting from the roof, and wrapping themselves around the building like a hug until there was nothing but green, glowing in the moonlight.

I ran all the way to Riley's house, explaining everything to Mrs. Owens the second she opened the door. I watched her face go from tired to serious as she realized the enormity of it.

"Where's Alex?" she asked, looking up the stairs. I shrugged and helped her search for him in vain.

Riley

The feeling of falling asleep was almost indescribable. I'll try anyway. It was like being late for school, but only having gotten one hour of sleep, and it's cold outside your warm bed. I could hear part of my brain yelling at me to get up, that this wasn't right. But my eyelids fought back, getting heavier and heavier until all I could see was black, and everything faded. I could still sense the ground shaking under me, but now it was comforting, like being rocked to sleep. *No* I screamed into the dark oblivion of the curse. There was no one to wake me up, no backup plan or safety net. I was on my own.

A mantra of words started to circulate through my head. *You don't need a prince to save you* trickled in and out of my mind, a blurry picture of a woman accompanying them. I strained towards her and the image crystallized for a split second, before it flew away to the corners of my subconscious that even a sleeping curse couldn't reach. I stopped fighting the dark.

Luke

Mrs. Owens finally gave up on the quest for Alex. "Maybe he's already there," she said hopefully, and I nodded supportively, even though I knew in my gut that we wouldn't find him anytime soon. "Now we wait," she added, sitting down on her couch and waving for me to join her. I shook my head, smiling with forced calm and backed away.

"My mom will be wondering where I am." I excused myself. She rested her hand against her forehead, too far gone to notice. I took that as a signal to go, and ran to my house. I grabbed the gun I had bought Riley as a birthday present that I never had a chance to give her and a sword that I had found hanging in Mr. Owens' closet when I was young. He had seen me eyeing it with admiration and had given it to me on a whim. I tucked the gun, on safety of course, into my back pocket, before tiptoeing back out of my mansion, sword held out in front of me.

The vines grew back twice as dense when I started slashing them, but I kept going, picturing Riley's lifeless body waiting for me upstairs. I stabbed until I was able to squeeze into the thorny overgrowth, sharp edges slicing my face and hands. The darkness surrounded me, and I used my phone as a flashlight, barely avoiding being skewered on a fully horizontal thorn. I found the door to the school, all the glass shattered and the wooden frames warped and broken. I could feel the hum of energy through the air, magic swirling around unburdened by the curse. A shot of light edged towards me and I backed away as well as I could before hitting the thorns behind me. Splinters of wood stuck into my arms when I pushed through the door into the main hall. The vines hadn't taken over yet, the building groaning and creaking as they expanded. I walked easily through the first set of doors into the stairwell. Seeing the roses twisted up and around the stairs, I let out a breathy swear and started hacking them away a step at a time.

Riley

I floated through the imaginary worlds as I slept. I dreamt of endless oceans and snowy banks with icebergs slamming together in a crackling ache. Something was still tickling the edges of my mind, a face appearing among the waves now and again. For the most part, I was alone, and I loved it. I wandered the corners of my brain, the incredibly realistic snow making me shiver. Suddenly, the ice shattered beneath me. I fell into the subzero water, sinking down, my limbs growing heavy from the wet and bitter arctic. The cold shocked me, jolting my head into overdrive. I could see his face again, across from me in the dark water. He had brown hair and green eyes. He disappeared again. I was the only one in the ocean, floundering desperately. Someone tapped my shoulder from behind, and I whipped around as quickly as my weighted limbs would allow. My mother was hovering above me, her perfect mouth curved up into a smirk as she watched my struggle. Alex materialized next to her, mimicking her sympathetically mocking expression. "You'll never make it," my mom said, her voice reverberating in the still water.

"You're going to die," Alex said pityingly. "You may as well give up now, princess."

"Who says I won't make it," I argued, able to speak in this bizarre underwater world.

"You're a girl," Alex said, his statement echoing his disdain.

"Girls are weak," my mom added, reaching out an impossibly long distance to stroke my cheek.

"No," I said firmly, and they exchanged sad looks.

"We didn't make the rules, darling," she explained, patting my hair. "That's just the way it is."

"No," I repeated, staring her down. "I make the rules. Not you, or Prince Asshole over here or anyone who doesn't have to live the rest of their lives as me." As I finished my sentence, I felt the ocean floor touch my feet, and I kicked off to where I could see light refracted in the swirling waves. I burst through the surface at the same time that I woke up, gasping for air.

My first reaction was *Oh shit what did I do?* as I slowly stood up, careful of the roses. But I raised my hand towards one, channeling the strict power I had felt during my dream, and it shrunk away from me. I turned towards the door, walking straight into the rapidly disappearing mess of branches and thorns. The vines, meant to protect me, had left deep cuts across my wrists and ankles, and any of my unprotected skin was stinging with incalculable scratches. Seemed like bad planning, really, as I could feel the droplets of blood forming over my eyebrows and on my lips, because honestly what kind of prince wanted his princess to be covered with blood? Good thing I didn't need a man to save me; in this state, I don't think anyone would want to kiss me. I limped to the entrance to the stairs, pausing to take a break before entering the stairwell. I turned the corner, panting, when I saw the flash of light and heard someone else climbing the stairs, his path about to collide with mine. I pressed myself against the wall, throwing out my fist when I estimated he would pass me.

"Ouch," Luke cried, retreating and almost falling back down the stairs if I hadn't grabbed his arm. "Riley!"

"Hey," I said, apologetically examining his face.

"You're awake," he said, pulling away in surprise. "So your mom was right. Alex was here."

"He was," I concurred bitterly, "but he's not the one who woke me up."

"Then who woke you up?" Luke frowned, an edge of jealousy spiking his voice—quite adorably I might add.

"I woke me up," I replied, raising my eyebrows in a dare to ask more questions and brushing past him.

"Fair enough," he said, hurrying after me.

The hallways were destroyed. The roses were sinking back into the ground, leaving no trace of any plants around, but the fractures to the school remained intact. The entire front wall had been cracked, leaving the school exposed and broken. Luke took my hand, leading me through the shattered glass to where the sun was starting to rise. "How long was I asleep?" I asked finally, checking my pocket for my phone and finding that a thorn had impaled it. Lovely.

"About six hours," he said, checking his watch, which was scratched but had survived. "Happy birthday," he added with a grin.

"Thanks," I grumbled, letting go of him to step outside into the weak but growing sunlight. The sun played over the glass dust that had been left covering my skin, making me glow. It also hurt like a bitch. I really needed a shower.

"That's a nice look right there," Luke joked, trying to take my arm again. His hand passed right through my glowing skin, and he held the appendage up, confused.

"Are you okay?" I said, reaching to touch his shoulder. My fingers brushed through his neck and he shivered.

"I don't think it's me, Rye," he answered, glancing at me in concern.

"What do you mean?" I asked, a hysterical bubble rising in the pit of my stomach. "No, no, no."

"Hey," he said, reaching out to comfort me and thinking better of it, "it'll be okay."

"You've said that so many times," I groaned, sitting down on the curb and putting my head on my arms. At least I could still touch myself, right? (Not what I meant guys, get your mind out of the gutter).

"And I'm going to keep saying that, until everything is, in fact, okay and then I can tell you that I told you so," he said, sitting down next to me, and his elbow sinking through me as he tried to put his arm around me and failed.

"Thanks," I grumbled, moving away from him and standing up. "By the way, this was the absolute most anticlimactic curse ever. I can't believe that I wasted four years of my life trying to stop something that I solved in six hours."

"I know," he said, shaking his head disbelievingly, "what's up with that? Talk about over preparing!"

"Let's go home." I sighed, gritting my teeth as I resisted the urge to hug him.

Luke knocked on my door for me, after I tried and almost fell through it. "Luke," my mom greeted him, after opening the door. She looked tired, and had to lean against the doorframe for support while she yawned. "Did you find Alex yet?"

"No," he answered, confused, "but I found Riley."

She looked straight through me to the direction of the main road. "I know, she's at the school, you already told me that." Luke and I looked at each other, my mouth tilting down. I waved my hand in front of her face with no reaction.

"Mom," I yelled, getting close to her face. Nothing.

"Oh, right," he said, giving me a nod to go. "I forgot. Sorry."

"No problem," she said with a drawn smile, "tell me if you find Alex please."

"I know where Alex is," I called back to her while she watched us, well Luke, go. "He's the asshole who did this. Don't expect me to marry him!"

"He did what?" Luke asked when we turned the corner and my mom was out of hearing range. I told him everything that had happened, from midnight on. He was turning red by the time I had finished, a murderous glint in his eyes. I tried to put a soothing hand on his arm, reminding me of the real problem at hand.

"Can we go fix this first?" I asked, cutting him off when he opened his mouth to start shouting profanities at wherever Alex was. He shut his mouth with a click and nodded, leading me to his house.

His mom couldn't see me either, which actually stung. I did learn that I could walk through doors though, because when Luke was the only person that Mrs. Moore could see, she slammed the door through me before Luke could stop her. It's a damn good thing that I wasn't a solid human because otherwise that would have hurt. Luke rushed to my aid, but I waved him off. "I'm fine," I said and laughed, sitting on the floor, unwilling to try to sit on the couch. Oddly enough, the floor was just fine, and I didn't sink through it to hang out with the worms or anything.

Luke explained my situation to his mom, while I curled up and tried to sleep. I gave up eventually, and watched Mrs. Moore listen attentively. When he was done, she sat next to me (I had to move back because Luke gave her bad directions and she sat on my head) and aimed a concerned look at where she thought I was. "Tell me exactly what happened during the curse," she directed, and nodded at Luke to translate.

"First I saw Luke," I started, waiting for him to relay it to his mom.

"Oh, so the thought of Luke woke you up?" she asked, looking through me.

"No," I answered. "I saw him but then he faded." Luke repeated that and I continued. "Then Alex came, and started being a jerk. And I was underwater, and I told my mom that I didn't need a man and then I saw the surface so I swam up to it and then I went into the light." She looked pensive, pondering Luke's words.

"You broke your own curse you mean," she said finally after a pregnant pause.

"You mean I'm practically a ghost because I solved my own problem for once?" I frowned. Luke reiterated the question, and she nodded, then shook her head, and then nodded again.

"You're not going to like this," she said, "but when you're

under the spell a fairly large piece of your soul goes on…hiatus shall we say. And then after true love's kiss, which solves almost anything, your soul would have come back. Since you woke yourself up, your soul never had the trigger to come back into your body."

"So I'm just a soul without a body right now?" I cried in horror.

She deliberated for a minute. "It does explain the 'not being able to touch you' part," she said slowly, tapping her lip thoughtfully. "In my opinion, the invisibility was caused by the physical action of breaking the curse. That takes serious magic, which is usually soaked up by love. Since you didn't have a boy or a girl to wake you up, the energy was taken from you, meaning anyone who was in the building at the time would be able to see you. So yes, your body is still in the school somewhere, but for now get some rest. You can always go back for it later."

"Thanks." I sighed, lying down again.

"Do you want to try and go upstairs?" Luke asked, sensing my uncomfortable position. "We have beds up there."

"Sure," I agreed, standing up. I tried to stand on a step but I went straight through it. "The floor's good, I guess." He tried to put a blanket on me when I went back to the carpeting, but that sunk through me too.

"I'm sorry," he said, looking as broken as I felt. I smiled through my trembling lips, trying to stay calm.

"It's fine." I laughed, ignoring the tears making my eyes itch. "I don't suppose you have a ground floor shower?"

"Is the water going to be able to touch you?" he asked pityingly.

"Good point," I said, blinking to get rid of the salt.

"Goodnight," Mrs. Moore said, and she and Luke left me to cry, curled up on the floor. At least only one person in the world could actually hear my sobs or see my makeup running, especially since I couldn't actually fix it. I fell asleep quickly. Sleeping for six hours was exhausting apparently, since that was all I'd done so far. Happy birthday to me.

Chapter Twelve

When I woke up, I still couldn't touch the blanket. I could hear Mrs. Moore humming in the kitchen, and stood up without much hope. I hopped around for a while, waving my hands around my head then running in circles to no avail. She still couldn't see me. I heard an amused chuckle coming from behind me and saw Luke, watching me with a smirk to rival my invisible one. "Seems like a great thing to do with invisibility," he commented, sitting down at his table and taking the soup his mom handed him.

"Is Riley here?" she asked, glancing around the room, her eyes finally landing on me. "Found you!"

"How?" I asked incredulously, Luke inquiring that at the same time so there was no need for translation.

"You're sparkling," she answered, nodded to the sparkles I was sending across the kitchen with my glass-covered arms. At least the sun could see me.

"Great, my girlfriend turned into a vampire overnight," Luke grumbled, taking a sip of soup. My stomach rumbled when I watched him. I tried to dip a finger in his soup, just to see if I could touch it, and scalded myself in the heat. I had honestly never been so happy to have a blister forming on my pointer finger. "Oh good, you won't starve," he said, trying to bat my hand away from his soup. "Get your own!"

"Here," Mrs. Moore said, setting a dish down on the floor with a spoon and a napkin. I reached for the spoon, and found that I could, in fact, hold it.

"Why can I touch these things and not everything else?" I asked, and Luke repeated it. This was getting seriously annoying. It was like having an echo.

"Thyme," she answered, nodding to the soup. "It has magical properties."

I nodded, mostly to myself for obvious reasons and took a careful sip of the soup, forcing myself to eat slowly in case of any weird curse side effects besides ghostliness and invisibility. "And before I forget," she added, pulling a pair of knitted gloves out of her pocket and throwing them at the air where she assumed I was. I picked them up cautiously, stroking the soft wool. "Special gloves soaked in thyme," she explained, sensing my confusion. I pulled them on and poked Luke in the face as a test, grinning as I made contact.

"Thanks, Mrs. Moore." I laughed, batting away his attempt at retribution before I remembered that it was only for my hands and let his hand pass through my nose.

Luke finished eating and sat down next to me, poking my arm. "I think you have to soak your fingers in thyme if you want to be able to touch me." I said, watching the borders of my arm shimmering and reappearing when he withdrew his hand.

"I know something that's soaked in thyme," he said and grinned, raising his eyebrows in a badly hidden innuendo. I leaned forward, touching his lips with mine. I am so glad that I didn't pass through his face. That's weird even for my life. Mrs. Moore cleared her throat when the kiss started to deepen.

"You understand how disturbing this is to watch, right?" she said. "You look like you're making out with air, Luke honey. This is worse than watching you kiss when I can actually see both of you."

"Oops." I blushed, pulling away from him. He smirked and leaned forward again, to where I had been. He started to move his lips in the empty air, imitating a fish taking gulps of water. "She's right." I giggled, watching Mrs. Moore's disgusted face and Luke simultaneously. "This is really weird."

"We could do so much more with your invisibility than this,"

Luke said, finally moving away from his fake invisible girlfriend.

"Whatever it is, you can do it at Riley's house." His mom sighed, and added, "your father is coming home in a couple of minutes."

"What?" I cried, shooting up. I had completely forgotten to watch the time. It was already past five o'clock; we had seven hours until the Special K could leave the forest, and I had focused on my own problems instead. "Special K," I yelled to Luke, pocketing the gloves and running down his front hallway to the door.

"Wait up," he called, hurrying after me. I ran through the door, not bothering to wait for him to open it. I am so lucky that my substance didn't return. The second that I hit the cold air, I could feel a shift in my stomach. I started shivering uncontrollably, staggering into the road. "Are you okay?" he asked, slowing to a walk as he watched me bent over. I threw up my lunch and paused to take a breath before doubling over again.

"Are you okay, miss?" a pedestrian queried, edging around the vomit.

"You can see me?" I said, gasping for air. She gave me a strange look and picked up her pace, muttering over her shoulder about drunks on Christmas Eve. "She could see me!" I grinned to Luke.

"I heard," he said, avoiding my lunch.

"Yeah." I groaned, straightening up and wiping my mouth. "I guess that's what it feels like to do a reverse disappearing act in the space of a minute."

"You can go home now at least," he offered, experimentally taking my hand. Nope, still ghostly material.

"Goody," I grumbled, turning left and crossing the street, a car going straight through me before I had realized. I flipped them off with my very noticeable finger. If I had hit a ghost I would have at least checked if they were okay. Undead have feelings too, you know. "Now I get to explain to my mom about all of this." I gestured to my body.

"She might understand," he said hopefully. She didn't.

101

My mom didn't stop yelling for at least twenty minutes. When she finally stopped, the house was silent. Everyone had been huddled in the living room, listening to our argument. As I entered the room again our distant relatives stared at me in wonder as one at a time they tried to give me a hug. At least avoiding unwanted affection was a bonus of this. The problem was that anyone that I actually wanted to touch would have to take a bath in thyme before they could hug me. I bet Luke would do that if I asked him to. Speaking of Luke, that coward had slipped out, rather than deal with the effects of my mother's wrath or my overly friendly family, leaving me alone with all of them. I couldn't even escape to my room, because at the point that I tried, and believe me I tried, I kept going through the stairs. Finally, I gave up, and walked through my front door. I found Luke sitting on the steps, staring into the entrance to our driveway. "What are we going to do about the Special K?" he asked when I sat down next to him.

"I don't know," I admitted, burying my face in my hands. "Your mom said that salt repelled them, maybe we should start with that?"

"Better than my plan," he said, standing up, and offering me a helping hand before he winced and withdrew it. "You'd honestly think that I would have realized that I couldn't touch you by now."

I laughed and shook my head. "Don't worry about it. It gets funnier every time that you forget because the idiocy increases."

"I feel like we're forgetting something," he commented when we were already halfway to his house.

"Well it better not be important because I don't want to walk all the way back... Wait!" I cried when I remembered. "We haven't told Jess any of this!"

"You're right." He groaned. "We're terrible people. I can't believe we forgot our third wheel."

"We are *not* calling her that." I frowned, looking both ways before crossing the street this time.

"Fine," he grumbled.

We found Jess (actually with her family on Christmas Eve. What a loser) and filled her in over the space of twenty minutes. "I can't believe how much I missed!" she cried when we had finished. "What the hell? Why did no one call me? We all have phones, we're rich white teenagers! I would have even settled for a text, like 'by the way, Riley's been cursed, you know, what we've been preparing for during the last four years, and her true love is evil. By the way, she's also invisible and untouchable but it's okay because if you touch soup you can poke her'!"

"We're sorry," I said, trying to give her a hug and going straight through her. (If you were wondering what the inside of a human body looked like, it's not pretty. I was a vegetarian for about a month after that.) Luke wrapped an arm around her for me.

"And now you come on Christmas Eve and tell me that the other thing, which we didn't really prepare for, is happening tomorrow, *on Christmas,* and you need my help, at seven o'clock at night on Christmas Eve to go pour salt in a forest which is harboring apocalypse starters?"

"Sounds about right," I confirmed. She glowered at me, or about as well as she could glower. She really was adorable.

"Fine," she snapped, going back inside her house and coming out with a canister of kosher salt. She pushed it in my direction but I illustrated the futileness by waving my fingertips through it vertically. "Right," she muttered, handing it to Luke instead.

"I think we might do better with that salt that they put on the roads when it snows," he said, giving it back to her.

"This is going to have to do," she said, shrugging. "We don't have any of that because we pay people to shovel our driveway and everything."

"Same," Luke and I said concurrently.

"This is why rich people are the first to die in apocalypses," I grumbled, leading them all the way back to my house. I strode through the door, not realizing that it was locked until I heard the doorbell ring.

"Get the door, won't you?" my mom called from the kitchen, looking down the hallway at me. I rolled my eyes largely at her, sticking my arm through the doorknob and back out. "Fine," she said, wiping her hands on her apron and undoing the lock.

"Thanks," Luke and Jess chorused, going straight to my kitchen. We found sea salt in the cabinet, in a plastic holder. Jess and Luke both took one of the jars and followed me outside to the edge of the woods.

The sun had long since set, meaning the outer ring of trees had already solidified into a wall. Luke started at one side of the woods, and Jess followed him, unwilling to be alone. He poured the salt in a steady line, a little thin but hopefully wide enough to work. We edged around the woods, through a shrub, which caused me to praise my lack of substance when I heard Luke and Jess swearing and struggling behind me, to the street. We caught some weird glances from passing pedestrians when he started to make a line of salt as close to the woods as he could, but after I walked through a few people they avoided us with the cool uncaring of rich people. Ah, the feeling of Christmas in the air. We hadn't even made it close to the beach when Luke ran out of salt. Jess took up his position, leaving no gaps in the line as she continued his work.

"What do we do now?" Jess asked, tipping her jar completely upside down to get the last grains of salt out.

"Shopping spree?" Luke and I grinned at each other and she rolled her eyes and shook her head disapprovingly but she was smiling too. We ran to the store together, (I was really appreciating my new lack of a body now, since I didn't have to look before crossing the street or open doors) and headed to the spice aisle. I pointed at which salt to grab, store brand mostly, because it was the cheapest, while they loaded the cart full. Luke paid for our small fortune in seasoning, the cashier giving us a very judgmental look but bagging our items all the same.

"Wait," I cried before the cashier handed Luke the receipt. I pulled on the gloves, running back to the spice aisle and grabbing four containers of thyme, carrying them back to the checkout line. I took the gloves off again before they ripped and I ended up with half a hand. The cashier arched an eyebrow but rang the spices up anyway.

"That must be some weird soup that you guys are making," she commented, clicking her tongue.

"The weirdest," I agreed, giving her a high five just to watch her face when her hand went through mine. It was priceless, by the way, if you were wondering.

We finished the lap around the woods, going back over the line that we had already done since we had more supplies.

"What do we do now?" Luke asked, after we had finished the second layer of salt.

"Now," I said, leading them back to my house, "we wait."

And at midnight on Christmas morning, the woods exploded.

At first the salt held. Every time a Special K hit the barrier, it sent a glowing dome around the woods. I felt cold metal being pressed into my hand and I jumped, afraid that I had gotten substance back in time for the goblin-pocalypse. I turned around and Luke was holding my gloves and a gun. I grinned over my shoulder, taking them and pulling on the gloves then aiming the gun. We could see the glowing fissures in the shield; maybe salt shouldn't have been our only plan. "Where's big boy?" I asked, hating the way that my voice shook.

"Maybe he decided to pass this up," Luke suggested, sounding more confident than I felt. "You know, send the minions ahead, and get some beauty sleep, all of those great factors."

"He definitely needs the beauty part," I said and laughed shakily, trying to keep my arm pointed towards the forest steady; I put it down after another minute because it was getting tired, raising it again whenever a new divide showed in our defenses. The glowing wall of magic from the salt was covered in Kallikantzaroi, more and more digging themselves up from the underground and joining the scrambling army. They climbed up each other, fighting for a spot. My old friends, stubby thumbs and moisturizer were at the front, and I swear I saw them staring at me. Soon, the rest of them stopped squirming and stood deadly still, focused on me.

"Guys?" I said, looking over my shoulder at Luke and Jess. They looked just as unnerved as me. Then, as if being controlled by puppet masters, the entire army looked up to the sky as a peal of thunder rang across the yard and it started to rain, even though it was like thirty degrees out and there was no actual reason for a thunderstorm to be happening in late December. The glowing wall hissed and sizzled as the salt began to dissolve and wash away.

"It's coming," Luke warned us, pointing his own gun at them. And sure enough, with a crash of lightning and an echoing scream, the wall was gone and the Special K were free. The first few that I shot melted into mud, no blood or bones left over as evidence. Jess threw handfuls of salt into the hoards as we backed away towards my house, causing the skin on them to bubble, and making them retreat with unearthly shrieking. The gun that I held became useless as rain started pouring down in sheets, shifting with the wind and blinding us.

"Run," I yelled to Luke and Jess, forcing them to back up. They glared at me in horrified indignation.

"We're not leaving you," Luke called back, centering his sword with a determined grimace. I threw my hands up in exasperation.

"They can't touch me! Flesh-eating goblins can actually hurt you two!" I cried, shaking my head desperately. They stood their ground and I rubbed my temple angrily. I closed my eyes, channeling the aftershocks of the curse into the full ire that I found while picturing my friends tied to a tree like Clayton.

My hands started to burn and I opened my eyes in surprise as tendrils of light crawled out of my fingertips and wrapped around Luke's arm. When his entire body was cocooned with the magic they started towards Jess, enveloping her in warmth. I watched in horror as my friends were slowly covered, their eyes reflecting my fear as they were slowly covered up. When nothing could be seen of them, the pure bright seemed to turn to me, as if waiting for instructions.

I hesitantly put my hands close to the shell holding Luke and it drifted towards me, humming with soothing goodness. It nudged my outstretched fingers and I studied it before I realized what it wanted.

106

"Oh, ok," I said. "Now for the hard part." I bit my lip, trying to decide where it would be safe to send them. I pulled two twenties out of my bra (in case you didn't know this, boys, that's where girls keep money when they don't have wallets. It's actually really handy) and parted the waves of glow with my hand until I found Luke. His eyes were closed and he was in a dead faint. "Even better," I muttered, unwrapping Luke's fingers from the handle of the sword that he was clutching and replacing it with money, curling his unmoving fingers into a fist.

I closed my eyes again, picturing Pittsfield, Massachusetts, from the one time I had been there to visit my aunt and uncle. "Good luck," I told them as the orbs started to spin in rapid tornadoes, before separating and dissolving like luminescent sandstorms. "God, I hope I didn't just kill my best friends," I said to myself, turning back to the advancing Special K who had been kept at bay by the magic, but had forgotten their fears. My leg started to tingle and I glanced down in distraction, freezing when I didn't see it. I brushed the missing appendage carefully, and felt pressure from both ends. "At least it's still there even if I can't see it, right?" I asked the oncoming goblins rhetorically.

They growled, (in agreement or not we'll never know) and with a tacit command they rushed the remaining distance towards me. It confused the hell out of them when the first few ran straight through me. I smiled at them, even though they weren't able to comprehend the sassiness of the situation, and sliced downwards, adding more mud to my backyard. I turned my attention back to the other Special K who were watching me with wariness now.

I walked through them, stabbing and cutting until piles of mud were littering the otherwise pristine grass. Some of them decided that being added as fertilizer wasn't worth it and started turning around before they left the safety of the forest.

I checked my watch: it was only half past midnight; I still had seven hours until sunrise and eleven, almost a full day until the town was safe. I sighed and turned around for any Special K that I had missed. The mud was reforming, twisting and solidifying to the wrinkled gray skin that we all knew and loved. "Why. Won't. You.

Stay. Dead?" I cried, punctuating each word by stabbing another goblin. "Come on," I snapped, watching them curl up to their old forms. "This has to end," I grumbled, walking though the scrambling forms to the end of the forest (I honestly have no idea who I was saying all of these things to).

They followed me, still trying to attack, and I stabbed down at them, more annoyed than anything else. I squeezed in between two trees (yes, now I realize that I didn't have to avoid them, thank you) and peered down into the fissure in the earth. It was pitch black inside, and when nothing jumped out to bite my head off I bent down to inspect it.

I turned the flashlight in my phone on and waved the narrow beam of light from wall to wall. The crack was extended maybe twenty feet long, scarring the forest where it had pulled up tree roots and broken tree trunks. It was shallow, and looked like I could easily stand in it while being able to reach the topsoil.

"What the hell," I muttered, pointing the flashlight straight down. It didn't exactly look like something that was a highway to the underworld. I didn't even feel the nauseated feeling that I had learned came with magic (if only I hadn't figured this out while throwing up my life would be complete). I leaned into it to brush my fingertips along the bottom, but I didn't feel anything. I sighed and pulled myself back up, considering my options in perplexity.

I crouched there, thinking, while the Special K ran around me in circles, stopping to try to bite me once in a while, which I ignored. Finally, I stood up and walked back to my backyard. I gave a rough estimate of how many there were, just to make sure that huge chunks of them hadn't escaped; it looked like they were all still there. I had only started with about two hundred anyway and the mud at the edge of the house that hadn't risen again was stopping them from going that way, while the wall of shrubs was trapping them on the other two sides.

I scanned them again, because if I couldn't kill them at least I could keep them here until sunrise. I'm not sure what happened, but I realized that I didn't see Stubby Thumbs or Moisturizer in the tumultuous masses. "Shit, shit, shit," I repeated into a mantra, pouring the leftover salt to make a neat line from one edge of my house to the shrubs and repeating on the other side to keep the others in. "Stubby, Moisturizer,"

I yelled, looking through the woods for them. I literally walked through the trees to the other side of the woods, calling out for them. I attracted other Special K but not the ones I wanted. I made it all the way to the beach without seeing them, and turned back. I checked the perimeter, but the only gap in the salt that had almost dissolved save for a dull white line in the dirt was in my backyard. I circled the woods again, stopping when I found another anomaly. "Weird," I said to the Special K who was standing on the other side of the line. He growled in agreement and stepped to my side of the line, trying to sink his teeth into my still visible leg. "Excuse me," I frowned, cutting his head off, "but that's the only leg that I can see. I'd like to keep it." I moved the pile of mud to the other side of the line before bending down again.

The salt line had been broken, but unlike the one in my backyard, which had exploded outward, this looked like it had been pushed in. Something had forced its way into the forest, and from what I could assume from the meandering Special Ks bumping into the barrier and looking for people to eat, it was probably a goblin. Something snapped in the dark behind me, and I whipped around with my sword raised, shooting into a standing position. The goblin that had made the noise gave me a crude smirk before melting into the side of a house.

I rushed after him, throwing salt at his body before he could kill whoever was in the house, and he dissolved. I grimaced in disgust as I picked up the mud and threw it in different directions, hoping to slow the creature down until I could figure out how to end this. I followed the trail of Special K, killing them and separating the mud all the way to Main Street. When I reached the intersection, I froze in horror. The little creeps were everywhere. I turned and threw up when I saw the remnants of my chemistry teacher on top of a car, her head on the hood and her body ripped open with goblins on top of her.

I wiped my mouth and stabbed them carefully, trying not to spear her body, even though she did give me a B last quarter. I heard a crash, and turned my head in time to see a handful of Special K crashing through a window of the electronics shop, examining themselves in the televisions that were programmed to project the security cameras. I sighed and crossed the street, sprinkling salt over them before they could hurt the cowering owner of the shop. He nodded his thanks and I waved, before running down the sidewalks to stop the goblins from throwing a car at a woman who was hiding behind a mailbox. "Buy salt," I advised her, giving her a hand up. "It keeps them away."

"Thank you," she gasped, hurrying in the direction of the grocery store.

"Pass it on," I yelled after her. I jumped into the street in time to pick up a little girl and keep her from being run over by a car covered in Special K who were trying to break in to get to the hysterical driver. I held her above my head as the car passed through me (thank god it was only a Prius; I'm not that tall), keeping her out in front of me, Lion King style, as I scanned for her mom. Finally, the woman ran up to me, sobbing, and I handed the daughter off, running after the car. I got to the goblins before they caused a car accident, giving the driver a handful of salt to keep him safe until he could get to the grocery store. My lungs were close to bursting when I made it back to Main Street and the dull ache of desperation as I watched another man fall victim to the never-ending army burned my eyes in tears. I bit my lip and sprinkled salt over him before they could destroy his body, moving on quickly. Why were all these fucking people out at one o'clock in the morning on Christmas?

"You!" someone shouted behind me. I spun on the spot, sword raised. "You were supposed to die," Alex said harshly, pushing my sword down with embarrassing ease. "You could have stopped all of this!"

Chapter Thirteen

Luke

I landed on my back on soft grass, jumping up and looking around. The fall had knocked the wind out of me, but the fall from where? I opened my hand that had been clenched at my side and money fell out. I picked two twenties off the ground, shaking my head to clear the confusion. I dodged what looked like a fast-paced gold cloud dropping from the sky, watching in awe as it condensed into Jess. She glowed for a split second before hardening back into flesh and dropping to the grass. She staggered, unable to catch her balance and I helped her upright. "Thanks," she squeaked, looking as dazed as I felt.

"Riley?" I asked, looking around.

"Riley," she agreed, pulling out her phone.

"Where do you think we are?"

"That's what I'm checking," she muttered distractedly, bringing up the phone's "Current Location" feature. "Pittsfield, Massachusetts," she read, looking surprised. "At least she didn't send us out of state."

"Riley gave us money," I offered, holding up the twenties.

"Please," she scoffed, pulling out a platinum card. "We're rich, remember?"

"Hey, if she's gonna send us a couple of towns away then the least we can do is spend her money," I argued, without any real conviction. I was too worried about what was going to happen if we weren't there to keep her from making dumb decisions.

"More than a few towns," she said, scrolling through a map of

Massachusetts. "It's at least three hours from here to Racheston."

"Three hours?" I cried.

She gave me an openly pitying look at the fear in my voice. "If Massachusetts is 190 miles long, and you're in a car driving 60 mph, so a mile per minute, it will take you three hours and ten minutes to get to Racheston which is on the coast. Pittsfield is closer to the border between Massachusetts and New York."

I glanced around us again. "It looks like we're in a park," I observed, still looking for the street. I followed the sound of honking horns to a main road where I flagged down a taxi.

"Where to?" the cabbie asked when we had gotten in.

"Racheston, please," I said, handing him the two twenties as incentive.

"You know it's going to be a lot more than this, kid," he commented, taking the money anyway.

"We know," Jess snapped, holding up the silver credit card. His eyes widened at the sight of it, and he floored the gas in a way that would have made me cringe if I hadn't been too busy thinking about Riley.

"We're coming, Rye," I murmured, as if she could hear me. Jess patted my hand comfortingly and stared out the window into the night.

"Merry Christmas," I heard the cabbie grumble.

Riley

"What do you mean I could have stopped all of this?" I cried, shaking my head in disbelief. "I tried, idiot, but nothing worked!"

"You were supposed to be the sacrifice," Alex continued as if I hadn't said anything. "If you had died, he wouldn't have let this happen."

"Who wouldn't have let this happen?" I asked incredulously, running a goblin through before it could jump on Alex.

"My dad," he yelled, getting in my personal space. I watched the spit fly through my face and praised the Lord for the millionth time that night that I had no substance.

"Your dad?"

He waved his arms widely. "He did this, Riley. He let the kallikantzaroi out from the underworld because the sacrifice," he gesticulated towards me, "that we promised him, *wasn't there!*" he finished, yelling the last two words.

"Oh, I am *so* sorry that I couldn't help you with that," I snapped, my voice heavy with syrupy sarcasm. "Wait," I interrupted him before he could retort. "Who's your dad?" He gave me a tired look, sitting down on the curb, and nodding towards the kallikantzaroi meaningfully. "No," I said, drawing out the word in disgust. "How old *are* you?"

"Younger than Sterling," he said and laughed mirthlessly. "I'm only one hundred twenty-six."

"Gross," I moaned, spitting on the ground. "I kissed someone who was alive for the beginning of World War I."

"What did you expect?" he asked sardonically. "My dad is the god of the underworld."

"So big boy is your dad," I reiterated in shock, shaking my head.

"Big boy?" he repeated, frowning.

"Apollyon," I explained, motioning that it was a story for another time if I resisted the urge to stab him. He nodded. "As much as I hate to ask this," I started, suppressing the images in my mind, "who's your mom?"

"Sterling's mom," he answered, looking at me in disdain like I should have figured it out.

"And who's that?"

"Ms. Sherton." He sighed, annoyed that I knew so little about my own town.

"Oh," I said thoughtfully, flashing back to the day of the happy housewives meeting. That actually made a lot of sense. "Go back to the sacrifice part," I said, standing up to stab a goblin before it could run through a window.

"My dad is fine with leaving this town to the hands of the mayor for a hundred years," he explained, dodging another kallikantzaroi. I threw salt on the goblin and aimed my attention back to him.

"Go on."

"Well," he said, eyeing a pair of Special K who were in turn watching us from across the street. I made sure that they were no direct threat and prompted him to continue with a sprinkle of thyme and a kick to his shin. He winced and glared up at me indignantly. "After one hundred years, the mayoral family is supposed to give up their oldest daughter to him as a sacrifice to show that they know he's the boss of the town. Your parents refused to do it, so Sterling and I took it into our own hands, because when my dad's unhappy, one of us is bound to be dragged down to the underworld to entertain him."

"My parents didn't want me to be killed?" I said, feeling somewhat special at least.

"Only 'cause your mom is too old to have another daughter and without the curse they would have to have an election," he scoffed. "In case you hadn't noticed, you're an only child."

"Oh," I deflated, thinking that that explanation actually made much more sense.

"Exactly," he smirked. Never had I appreciated those gloves more than when I slapped the smile off his face, grinning when he tried to hit me back and fell straight through me, landing face first on the pavement.

"I'd say that you shouldn't hit girls, but then I wouldn't be able to hit you," I jeered as he scrambled to his feet.

"What the hell?" he said, waving his hand through my face.

"The price of magic is high when your prince is an asshole." I smiled sweetly, enjoying the look on his face more than I should have.

"Right," he said. "You should have died."

"Are we back to this?" I said unhappily. "I could have died, or you could have killed your dad in his sleep, so we're both at fault."

"I guess," he agreed, with a smile that looked like it was a grimace of frustration that he couldn't kill me himself.

"So what do we do?" I asked before he could actually take any action.

"Now we fight," he said, running into an abandoned convenience store, and coming out with a knife. He stabbed a passing kallikantzaroi, watching it melt into mud with a mix of disgust and nauseating pride.

"What do you think I've been doing?" I groused at him, slashing at two goblins at once. "I was hoping that you'd have a more permanent

114

solution."

"Survive until the end of the twelve days of Christmas?" he suggested, cutting down a goblin that was trying to climb the telephone pole after a bird.

"Twelve days?" I cried, momentarily distracted.

"You didn't know that?"

"No!" I said, horrified. "The book said that I only had to survive until the day after Christmas! How am I supposed to keep all these people alive and my friends from coming back?" I gestured to the surrounding houses and shops in wild apprehension.

"You don't," he answered shortly. "You fight, and if you live then you help rebuild the town. That's what happened last time too."

"You were here last time?" I said, examining him out of the corner of my eye.

He nodded and shrugged. "I was twenty-six, and I was married here."

"You were married?" I repeated. This story kept getting better and better.

"To the mayor's daughter." He smirked, and suddenly I realized it was just a ploy to get her to kill herself. I recoiled in anger, pretending to aim for a kallikantzaroi but "missing" and slicing his arm instead. "Hey!" my fragilely allied companion said, glaring at me.

"Sorry," I said, with a smug look of my own. "Carry on."

"My dad made me do the same thing that I did to you," he continued, still glowering as the blood ran rivulets down his wrist. "I showed up and told her that I was her true love, and since it was 1914, she believed me. It was a more romantic time," he explained, "and she wasn't as smart as you. Plus, feminism wasn't really a driving force in her life," he added nostalgically. "It was a simpler time."

"So what happened?" I prompted, scanning the area for any more people in danger. The farther along the road that we walked, the more frequent that the salt circles became, and I felt a swell of pride that the first few people had heeded my advice and passed it along as well.

"I courted her," he said, "then I tried to lure her into where my dad was going to split the earth. But her dad figured out my game and tried to kill me, so I ran. I came back, just to see what had happened to the town, and it was burned to the ground. No survivors." I shivered at his last words and looked behind me to see the Special K rising back to their true forms.

"Well, that Racheston didn't have me," I said, determinedly, and he rolled his eyes.

"I hope you're not this stubborn when you're dead," he muttered to himself, but I managed to catch the briefly admiring glance that he threw me.

"Thanks," I smiled cheerfully, running full tilt into a crowd of clamoring goblins.

Chapter Fourteen

Luke

My leg jiggled in anticipation while I stared out the window at the blurring highway. The stretch of road was empty; I wasn't surprised that no one else wanted to drive anywhere at two o'clock in the morning on Christmas. We had been driving for an hour, and at the promise of an extra large tip, the taxi driver hadn't let the speed dip below 80 mph. At this rate, it would take another hour and forty minutes to get to Racheston. "Can you go any faster?" I asked, and he shot me a dirty look in the rearview meter, but pressed the gas pedal down as far as it would go anyway. I felt the jolt of extra velocity and beside me Jess groaned. She was turning green from the incredible pace that we were racing down the road at, and it was my turn to pat her hand soothingly. "We'll get there faster this way," I told her, and she nodded like she was afraid to open her mouth.

"I don't think we'll be any help to Riley if we're dead by then, though," she croaked.

"So is your friend in trouble or something?" the cab driver said without any real interest spiking his voice.

"We're worried that she's going to do something stupid without us," I replied, envisioning all of the ways that she could die if we weren't there to stop it. I let out a moan of my own and slumped back against the seat, visions much less comforting than sugar plums dancing in my head. Merry Christmas to all, and to all a crappy, crappy night.

Riley

I honestly didn't think that I'd ever spend an hour fighting side by side with someone that I had punched, not once but twice, but as the clock ticked closer to quarter-to-three, I had to admit that Alex was a good person to have on my team.

We stood back to back, stabbing and scattering mud wherever we could, but mostly drawing as many salt circles as we had the supplies for. I had used my magic again, twice: once to kill a kallikantzaroi from across the street when I saw that it was posed to kill an insomniac jogger, who screamed in terror and ran for his life, and once to reproduce the salt that we had left, since we were too far from the store to double back. Now I couldn't see my left hand or my other leg. I must have looked like an extremely wounded ghost to any bystanders, and I nearly tripped every time that I glanced down at my legs before remembering that they were both there. I could barely stand as it was, my unfortunately invisible ankles shaking from exhaustion. We sat down every ten minutes, unable to go on, and after the fourth time that we did this I burst into tired tears.

Alex tried to pat my shoulder in the awkwardly comforting way of boys, but I buried my head in my arms, wiping my eyes and my nose on my shirt. "Lovely," he commented, watching me do this.

"Thanks," I replied, grinding the heel of my hand into my eye to keep it open. I fell asleep briefly, curling up on the sidewalk until Alex told me in an equally tired voice to stand up. I looked up, and saw a line of kallikantzaroi advancing on us, growls building in their collective throats. I checked my watch: three-thirty. "I don't suppose these things are afraid of sunlight," I sighed, drawing my sword again.

"They thrive on it," he replied. "They only get it once every one hundred years. They must be seriously deprived of vitamin D." I grinned at his joke, sobering up when the kallikantzaroi rushed us.

"But really," I said, stabbing through four goblins. I was getting good with this sword. "What happens to them in the sunlight?"

"They retreat to the forest," he said, with just as much seriousness, "and they come back out the second that the sun starts setting."

"So we have about four more hours of fighting, and then less than twelve hours of a break?" I summarized, despaired.

"Pretty much," he agreed, pausing the wipe a trickle of blood from his mouth.

"This has to end," I decided, cutting off a goblin's head before it could sink its teeth into him. "I'll do whatever it takes."

Luke

We were five minutes away from Racheston, and Jess had already thrown up four times out the window. "If you puke in my cab you pay for it," the driver growled, lighting a cigarette in a stereotypical city way. "I'm already driving you across the state on Christmas." We didn't even wait for him to completely stop the cab before jumping out to the pavement. I sprinted into the town, not waiting for Jess to finish paying him. She swiped her credit card, signing off on the amount, $540.60 plus an extra $100 as a tip, and ran after me.

"Where would she be?" I asked desperately, turning circles on the town line.

"Check her backyard," Jess suggested. We practically flew to her house, where the number of trapped kallikantzaroi drove us away to the center of town. It was deserted besides the goblins running rampant, but there were the telltale piles of mud, making a trail going up to the school.

"Oh no," I moaned, falling to my knees when I saw it. If she went back into the school, she would regain her substance. What if she was attacked in her actual body? How was she supposed to survive an army of goblins and an evil prince without us?

Riley

"You're willing to die for this town?" Alex repeated in shock, almost getting hit with a kallikantzaroi, but moving to the side just in time.

"Whatever it takes." I nodded. "One life, compared to the death of this entire town isn't worth it."

"If you're sure," he said warily. I nodded again and I saw something flicker in his eyes. He set his jaw. "Okay. Let's do this."

We walked up to the school, shoulder to shoulder. He led me through the shattered doors, across the rippling floor and followed the shaking walls to the stairs. I banged my shin on a fallen doorframe, gritting my teeth against the swear bubbling to my lips and focusing on the positive instead. At least I had substance again, just in time to die. The earthquakes were getting stronger the closer that we drew to the chemistry room, to the point where I had to stop because I couldn't feel my legs. He took my hand to give me support. His hand was trembling worse than mine as the dread of what we were about to face set in. "You got her to come," Sterling's maliciously cold face greeted us when we made it up the stairs.

"She came on her own," he answered through gritted teeth.

"Whatever." She shrugged, making way for us.

"You don't have to do this," he muttered in my ear, his eyes pleading. I gave him a strange look and he continued. "We can fight this together, Rye."

"Don't call me that," I said, pulling away from him and walking towards the middle of the room.

"Fine," he replied, his eyes hardening. "Do it," he said to Sterling.

"Wait!" I cried, catching sight of my body, which had been covered in dust and dragged to the corner by someone. It had been propped up into a sitting position with my dulled eyes open. I shivered as I examined it; the completely blank look on its face gave me goose bumps. I rid myself of the gloves, reflecting my body's exact pose and falling backwards into it. I woke with a start from the brief moment of darkness accompanying the transaction and sneezed reproachfully. If someone had taken the time to prop me up I don't see why they couldn't have dusted me off too. "You're good," I told Sterling, waving for her to start.

She nodded with a calmly creepy smile and raised her hands above her head. "Father," she called in a clear ringing voice. The ground shook in response, the intact windowpanes rattling. She took this as a sign to continue. "We feel your presence, we know you're here," she chanted, waiting for Alex to join in and shrugging again when he didn't. "We aim to please, we know what you want. We want to give you happiness, and we know your happiness comes in the form of a sacrifice." She paused for dramatic effect, then said, "Open your doors to let in your sacrifice!"

The tiled floor exploded upwards, showering us in shrapnel. I was thrown to the floor, wincing when my head hit the corner of the wall. I sat up, breathing heavily and using the wall as support, warm blood trickling down the side of my face into my hair. That was going to be a pain to wash out. I pushed myself off the wall, noticing the effects of the force of the eruption.

Luke

I left Jess far behind me as I sprinted to the skeleton of the school, each step becoming a word. *Please don't let it be too late*, I repeated through my mind at every pounding footstep. I took the stairs two at a time when I got to them, and what was waiting for me at the top took my breath away.

Chapter Fifteen

Riley

I was covered in dust, and my arm was hanging out of the socket. I used the wall as support, picking up the sword from where it had landed next to me and dragging myself into a standing position. Across the room, Sterling had been knocked unconscious and Alex was shaking his head to clear it, but they seemed otherwise unharmed, unfortunately.

I staggered towards the hole in the floor, pausing every time my arm moved a millimeter and pain shot through my shoulder. I peered over the edge, expecting to see the bottom floor of the school at least, since we were on the second level, but all I could see was darkness. I picked up my phone and pocketed it, giving the power button a testing squeeze. It turned on, despite the thorn-sized hole through the center. I bit my lip to keep from showing the pain, even though I was sure that it was written on my face, and turned the flashlight on. The effort of holding it up became too much for my aching body, and it fell from my hand with a hiss into the darkness. I leaned farther over the edge, watching the fading light with a wave of regret until I remembered that I was going after it, and then I didn't feel so bad about the waste of a perfectly good phone.

Alex was watching me from the door, a surprisingly aching expression on his lips. "Let's do this," I said, with a brave smile. He shook his head pleadingly, coming forward and grabbing my hand.

"Please, Rye," he said. "I had such a good time fighting with you tonight that I wouldn't mind doing it for another twelve days." I sighed and looked back to the swirling vortex under our feet. I could see the clouds of smoke rising out of it, more mysterious than I expected them to be.

"Thanks for not being a complete asshole in the end," I said, kissing him lightly on the cheek. He froze at the gesture, tightening his grip on me. I wrenched my hand away gently, teetering on the edge with bated breath.

"No!" someone yelled from the doorway, and I turned my head towards the sound. Luke was staring at me with the distraction of a man on the brink of losing life itself.

"Luke," I said, taking half a step away from hell to face him. "I thought I sent you to Pittsfield!"

"You did." He panted, moving into the room, giving Alex a wide radius and reaching out for me. I immediately went into his arms, kissing him with hopeless fervor and pushing him away again.

"Don't do this," I said, feeling my lip tremble as I heard the mirrored chord of heartache. "It'll make everything so much harder."

"Good," he said angrily, stepping towards me. I could sense the lack of space behind me. A sneeze could send me over the edge at this point. I held my breath again, trapping it in my chest until I could feel it getting stale and exhaled slowly. I held up my good arm to stop him, and he paused. "Come back to me," he said quietly, with the tender resonance of hurt. Two tears spilled over my cheeks as I thought about it. Fighting would be worth it with Luke by my side.

"Time's up," Sterling snapped, to the left of me. She twisted so that she could knock Luke out of the way, giving me a hard shove and throwing me off balance. I stepped backwards onto air, grabbing her wrist as I fell, tumbling through the cold deep with the feeling of dread building stronger in my stomach the farther into the earth that we followed my phone. I lost track of the time, until finally the intensity of the blood pounding in my head caused me to pass out and not wake up until we had landed.

123

Luke

I lunged forward towards Riley as she fell, missing her by mere inches. "No, no, no," I muttered to myself, rocking forward on my heels when a sob ripped through my chest. The darkness enveloped her until nothing was left but the echoing surprise that she had let out in a gasp. Alex was staring at the pit in surprised horror when I rounded on him, pulling my arm back and letting it snap back into his face. He didn't even flinch at the impact; he was still staring at the pit. "Missing Sterling?" I asked sarcastically.

"Her going is the only good thing that's come out of this," he replied coolly.

"You like Riley," I said in a brief moment of clarity. He nodded once in response, a guarded wrinkle between his eyebrows.

"Whatever it takes," he muttered to himself, brushing past me and stepping into hell. Refusing to be shown up by a guy who was in love with my girlfriend, I jumped in after him.

Riley

Hell was a lie. There were no flames surrounding me when I woke up, no Devil with a pitchfork and no screams of the suffering. The ground felt almost gravelly, but when I found the strength to open my eyes all I could see was a thick slab of stone under me. I curled up to a sitting position, looking around me. I was in a room made of cement and granite, the walls painted a frightening shade of indigo. My mouth tasted like sawdust, and I spit onto the ground to get rid of it. I heard a moan coming from the opposite side of the space, in the shadows that shouldn't even had existed without a discernible light source. Sterling was waking up in the corner.

I rolled off of my back onto the balls of my feet, stretching my legs until I was standing. I spotted my phone that had somehow survived the fall too (admittedly good quality. A great phone to have if you're ever stuck in a psychopath's plan of thorns and sacrifice). Sterling watched with deadly amusement as I pounded on the walls, tracing every imperfection in the stone hoping to find a door. "Daddy doesn't make these rooms so that people can escape you know," she commented after my fifth lap around the room.

"Well I was hoping that I wouldn't actually wake up," I snapped, glaring at her from a distance. Her brown eyes seemed to glow red.

"It wouldn't be a sacrifice if it was easy darling," she smirked, stretching languidly and yawning.

"Thanks," I grumbled, choosing to ignore her. "You're not the least bit worried about dying?"

"Dad would never hurt me." She smiled, but I noted with satisfaction the sparkle of fear that moved at light speed through her features. She was as uncertain as I was about the future. Good.

"I would hurt you if I was your dad," I said, pushing on one of the walls. It remained unmoving and frustratingly solid rock. "Now what?" I asked her, giving up and plopping down at the center of the room.

"Now," she said, "we wait."

Luke

Hell was not what I had imagined. I guess I hadn't really thought about dying as much as I should have, but I was kind of hoping that I was going to go to heaven if anything. The few times I had thought about the opposite end of the spectrum, I had pictured it like the Bible described it: some nice burning souls, flames as tall as skyscrapers, those kinds of things. I had been knocked out by the pure velocity of hurtling towards the center of the earth, and had been woken up by my less-than-graceful landing.

Alex hit the ground next to me, bounced, and settled back down. The earth under our feet was an uninviting shade of black that looked like it had been chopped up in a blender with tires and diamonds, creating a shimmering spongy surface. There weren't trees, but the earth was raised in some places where the tips of pearly bones had begun to rise, and in the more matured "plants" the tangle of femurs and tibias made the appearance of a bush. Depressing, but not what I thought hell would look like.

"My dad needs a better interior decorator," Alex groaned as he sat up, like he had read my mind.

"I do like the lack of suffering souls," I said optimistically. "Whoa." I had turned in a one-eighty and finally noticed the granite castle that looked like it had been pushed forcibly out of the earth. "Is that where your dad lives?"

"I guess." He shrugged. "This place has changed from the last one hundred years that I was here."

"How old are you?" I asked incredulously.

"Hundred twenty-six," he answered, standing up and brushing the diamond sparkle off of himself.

"And you're still trying to steal my girlfriend?" I frowned. "Aren't you a little old for her?"

"I've taken the years well, wouldn't you say?" he replied, gesturing to his face, and tilting his head so the eerie light danced across his cheekbones. But his eyes held mine in an ancient sadness and I felt a wave of guilt; clearly, I had struck a nerve.

"Dermatologists must hate you," I agreed, relaxing when I saw him grin out of the corner of my eye. "Now come on, we have a girl to rescue."

"It would be a miracle if she hasn't already done something stupid and gotten herself killed," he said, moving past me and walking into the castle.

"Alex," I hissed after him, "what are you doing?"

"If my dad is the king of the underworld then I'm the prince, right?" He kept on strolling down the hallway with an undeniable swagger that stopped the silent servants passing us to stare for too long. He practically belonged here. He only shuddered to a stop when we heard a booming echo of a voice at the end of the passage. "That's my dad," he said, searching for somewhere to hide.

"He won't hurt you, right?" I asked, joining him.

"It's not me that I'm worried about," he snapped, and we ran back the way we had come until we found a door. He ushered me inside, closing us in with a sharp click. The inside of the room was pitch black and I fumbled along the edge of the wall for a light switch until I remembered that we were in the underworld. "Here," he said, clapping his hands together. An orb of light flickered on, shedding a short circle of light around us.

"Wait," I said, pulling my phone out of my pocket. The front screen was cracked, but when I pressed the power button I could see the telltale muted glow. I turned the flashlight feature on, waving it around the walls. I took a tentative step forward, something cracking under my foot.

"Down," Alex yelled, dragging me to the ground as a blade whistled over my head and embedded itself into the wall in front of me.

"Thanks, man," I said, lifting my head.

"My pleasure," he replied, standing up and taking the phone out of my hand. "Nice," he sighed sarcastically, pointing the beam of light to the walls again. I noticed a small passage between the solid stone facing us, creating the look of a doorway, and beyond it more stone.

"Where are we?" I said, staring transfixed at the blade, still quivering in the wall.

"The maze of pain," he said cheerfully.

"Please tell me that your dad thought he was being funny when he named this and that this maze is actually incredibly easy and gives us hot chocolate at every corner," I said then groaned, alternating between looking at his face and then back to the knife.

"It's easy if you know what you're doing," he allowed. "Which you don't."

"But you do, right?" I studied his rapidly darkening face.

"Unfortunately," he said, taking a step forward into the waiting darkness. "You coming?"

"Unfortunately," I repeated, following his exact movements.

Riley

After another ten minutes, I couldn't take it anymore and stood up again. I felt Sterling's gaze burning into the back of my head and my shoulder blades stiffened unwillingly. "What," I snapped, not turning around.

"What did you do to Alex?" she said, so quietly that I felt a spark of interest.

"Why do you care?"

"Because he's my brother and I don't want to see him get hurt," she answered coldly.

"I didn't do anything to Alex," I replied, still examining the wall with my head held high.

"Bullshit," she muttered, but let it go.

"Open up," I said to the wall, frustrated by its solidity. When it did nothing, I punched it with my good hand, regretting it immediately. The burn of a broken knuckle danced through my hand, and I gritted my teeth.

"Nice," Sterling smirked from behind me and I painfully flipped her off.

"Shut up, you're not even trying to do anything," I said angrily.

"My dad would never hurt me," she replied sweetly.

"Then why would he keep you trapped in this room?" I asked, turning on her.

"Maybe he doesn't know I'm here," she argued.

"Right," I snorted, running my good (actually just better) hand along the wall again. Where I had punched it, it had cracked, a ragged fissure about a foot long. I focused my energy on it, before I remembered that any magic in the underworld might trap a piece of my soul here. I guess we were doing this the old-fashioned way.

I picked up my sword that had fallen, point down next to Sterling (thank god it hadn't stabbed me; they warn us against running with scissors, but no one told me not to fall to a different dimension with an unsheathed sword) and jammed it into the wall. The first time it just bounced off, but the second time I got it directly into the widest section and pried. Another piece of rock crumbled away and I cheered, forcing the sword back in again and again. Before long, I had a gap in the unbending rock, big enough to fit my hand into. I dropped the sword and wrenched at the loosened rock, tears streaming down my face as the dull ache in my shoulder sharpened.

"Some help?" I directed to Sterling, who sighed and stood up. I braced my foot against the wall and gave a rough yank at the same time as Sterling, and a brick the size of my torso was pulled out. The darkness beyond was unending, where I had expected to see flames or something hellish. "Are you coming?" I asked her. She was backing away from me slowly.

"Into the maze of pain? Are you *crazy*?"

"Maze of pain? Why do you look scared? That sounds so inviting," I drawled, shimmying through the opening and dropping to the other side.

"Good luck," Sterling said, throwing me down my sword, "but you're on your own." Her head disappeared from the hole with a final nod, leaving me to take slow steps into the darkness, with one good shoulder, no good hands, and no friends.

Chapter Sixteen

Luke

Alex and I were forced to hold hands in the darkness to keep from separating. "Bro, no homo," I said, refusing to lace our fingers together.

"We're never speaking about this to anyone else, agreed?" he said, obviously embarrassed.

"Agreed." I nodded, my face turning red. We had noticed, after about the fifth knife whistling past our ears, that the tiles to avoid all had the same subtly swirling pattern across the face of them, often unnoticeable until we had to duck. We had to turn around six times after hitting dead ends, making the maze twice as dangerous because we had to figure out which tiles not to step on for the way back too. "How far are we into the maze?" I asked after what I assumed was about an hour. I didn't know for sure because my phone was stuck at three forty. Apparently, the underworld didn't have Standard Eastern Time.

"Not even halfway," he said and sighed, looking around us to all the walls that looked exactly the same. "And we don't even know that Riley is in the center, she could be in a different part of the castle."

"Great," I said, with as much cheer as I could muster. Alex shot me a disgusted look. I glared back at him until a growl from the walls in front of me made me turn around. The skeleton of a lion stalked us from the doorway of where we had to go.

"Back away," he instructed, under his breath. "We'll go around." We didn't have a chance to move, because at the twitch of our chests as we inhaled, it lunged. We reacted immediately, splitting apart and diving to separate sides of the room. It paced back and forth, clearly doing "eenie meenie miny moe" in his missing brain. I searched the room desperately for a weapon, my eyes falling on a familiar patterned tile.

"Duck," I advised Alex, who caught my eye knowingly and nodded. I pressed the tile, catching the handle of the knife with sheer luck, and stabbing down at the spine of the lion when it lunged. I missed, hitting his neck instead and his head popped off. The body crumbled into dust, and I stood back up shakily. I helped Alex get to his feet, taking his hand again wordlessly, and avoiding his eyes.

"Good job," he said gruffly, ignoring our attachment.

"Thanks." I coughed, trying to sound as manly as I possibly could.

"Let's go find Riley," he suggested, stepping over the still growling skull into the empty passageway. I nodded wordlessly.

Riley

The first real problem I came across was in the form of a pit. I had already found the tile that threw knives at me, and knew to avoid stepping on anything that looked like it had vines squirming across it. In my quest to avoid those stones, I accidently skipped onto a tile with an X on it, which I probably shouldn't have. I had to launch myself off it, rolling onto my back and into a standing position. The ground crumbled away, falling into a void in the earth. I caught my breath, using the thankfully solid wall as support. The entire room had fallen into the darkness, and I had to use the wall as a guide while I shuffled along the edge, legs shaking. I paused when I kicked a piece of gravel into the pit, listening for a clatter as it reached the bottom that never came. I picked up my pace after that, stretching my leg as far as it would go to the safe (safer) ground. I practically ran to the next room when I heard something in the pit let out a snore and a shuffling sound.

I only had to turn back twice, after hitting a room with no exits. I wasn't sure that punching the bricks would work again, and doubling back seemed a little easier. I wasn't sure how long I had been in the maze; the clock on my phone was broken. My vision was blurring from exhaustion and I had run out of adrenaline from when I had started. I couldn't go on without at least a nap. I tried to recall the last time that I had slept, but my memories were fuzzy around the edges, only catching sections of faces and a few words. It was probably just a side effect of not sleeping for however long it had been. I curled up in a dark corner, hoping that nothing would happen on this room and eat me. I closed my eyes and immediately fell asleep.

Luke

I had to catch Alex again as he stumbled to a stop. He looked dead on his feet. "You need sleep, man," I said, letting him slide down the wall into a sitting position.

"We need to find Riley," he insisted, trying to get back up.

"I hate to tell you this but you're slowing the operation down a little bit," I said, keeping one hand on his head so that he couldn't get up.

He stopped struggling, letting out a soft sigh that sounded almost like "oops" before falling fast asleep. I watched him for a little bit, fighting my heavy eyelids, before watching both doorways at either side of the room. I leaned against the wall for a while, tilting my head back to look at the ceiling. I couldn't see anything in the darkness, which was creepy but not as bad as when red eyes started staring back at me. I glanced down at Alex, who was sleeping peacefully, then back up at the eyes. They blinked slowly, waiting for my move. I nudged Alex with my toe, not breaking eye contact with the ceiling. He shifted in his sleep but didn't wake up. I kicked him again, harder this time, and heard him groan. "What?"

"What has eight red eyes and sticks to ceilings?" I muttered to him.

"I give up, what?"

"I don't know, but I don't think we're going to like it," I answered, pulling the knife out of my belt. He followed my gaze all the way up to the ceiling.

"We're definitely not going to like it," he agreed, picking up the knife that was lying next to him and standing up with slowly precise movements.

"Do we risk making a break for it?" I asked, judging the distance between the door and us.

"On three," he breathed. "One." We braced ourselves. "Two." I shifted the weight onto my front leg. "Three," he said and we sprang into action. The thing dropped to the ground with a screech, blocking Alex's path. It was a spider, easily twice our size, with two pinchers as thick as my arms and razor sharp. Alex dove to the side as the spider lunged, motioning for me to go on. I shook my head wildly.

"Hey!" I shouted to the spider. It scuttled around so it was facing me. "How's it going, man?" I said, watching Alex edging around it out of the corner of my eye. The spider started moving toward me, shifting back and forth on its thick legs. It clicked its pinchers and I waved my knife. "I wouldn't do that if I were you," I told it, trying to sound confident in my abilities to kill a spider that would take up half of an Olympic sized swimming pool. It didn't heed my warning and sprang at me anyway. I dodged to my left, slicing towards its head, and feeling the impact. The spider squealed and retreated, silvery blood running down the left side of its face.

"Let's go," Alex called from behind me and I backed into the new room. "Thanks," he said when we were sure that the spider wasn't following us.

"All in a day's work." I laughed, grimacing as I wiped the spider blood on the ground. "That's disgusting."

"Your turn to sleep if you want it," he offered, stepping away from the spider blood and motioning toward a corner. "I promise I'll wake you up if the giant spiders attack."

"Thanks," I said, lying down on the cold ground and tucking my arms under my head. I drifted off to sleep, dreaming of the Christmas we had missed and wondering if the goblin-pocalypse had been stopped yet.

Mary Quinn

Jess

I watched both of my best friends die on Christmas. I had been too far behind Luke, taking the stairs one at a time like a human and trusting him to save Riley. By the time that I made it to the chemistry room, the pit to hell had already opened. The roar of it was too loud, and I couldn't hear what Luke was saying to Riley, but something made it through her stubborn mind because she had started to step away from the hole in the floor. I called out to her when Sterling woke up, but I was too late. Luke stared in horror at where Riley had been, watching Alex follow her down. I rushed forward as Luke jumped in too, but the hole sealed and I was left with smooth tile.

I dropped to my knees, searching for a crack or any sign of where my friends had gone. I wrapped my arms around my knees, trying to stifle my sobs. What the hell was I going to tell their parents? I sat there for an hour, trying to breathe evenly. When I was sure that they weren't coming back I let out a choppy sigh. At least they were together. Between the two of them they had a chance of making it out of hell. I left the school slowly, trying to find a weapon to fight the goblins with now that I was on my own. When I got outside, the town was empty. I wandered through Main Street, looking for any sign of the little monsters, but the only evidence that there had been a war here were the cracked windows and piles of mud that hadn't risen again. I felt a surge of pride for my friends; they had done it.

Chapter Seventeen

Riley

I woke up slowly, blinking the sleep out of my eyes as I waited for the memories to come rushing back. I stood up carefully, trying not to touch any other bricks in the floor. I yawned and shook my head to clear it. I felt much better than I had last night when…when what? I couldn't remember what I had done last night. I bit my lip, searching the bare edges of my thoughts. I could feel the ebb and flow of the memories, and breathed a sigh of relief when they flitted back. I was here to save the world, to find my boyfriend and kill a king and get out of here.

I stretched and turned my phone on to use the flashlight. "No, no, no," I muttered when the low battery sign flashed across the screen and it turned back off, "you can't leave me too." Apparently, it could leave me as I watched it die; I was officially on my own. The blackness was choking me, constricting my throat with fear and clenching my hand tighter around the sword. What was worse: risking loss of soul or getting decapitated with one wrong step? "Maybe the King of the Underworld can afford every room lighting," I said and then laughed to myself, clapping like we did at our house to turn the light on. To my utter surprise a ball of light appeared, bobbing welcomingly. I reached up to touch it and it darted out of my grasp. "The King of the Underworld has good taste," I commented to the light, mentally christening it Bob. "Let's go Bob," I ordered, stepping carefully into the next room. Bob followed me willingly, even when I had to retrace my steps to a different room.

135

"You're my only friend, Bob," I told him. He seemed to nod in agreement.

I started to sing under my breath after a while as I got bored of the same scenery over and over. I began with "Hot-Blooded" by Foreigner, because it seemed fitting for hell, but then I remembered that this was a Goth and depressing hell, and I sang "Cold As Ice" by them instead. My songs slowly started to crescendo after a couple of hours, until I was practically yelling "Eye of the Tiger".

I shut my mouth with a click after I heard a hiss and remembered that I was in a maze designed to cause pain and suffering. It was too late; I'd had already attracted something.

"Why didn't you tell me that this was a bad idea?" I asked Bob accusingly. He ignored me. "Whatever," I told him as the doorway was expanded forcefully as something large tried to find me. I jumped out of the way of some flying stones, rolling under the giant snake that had caused the explosion and was trying to wriggle the rest of its body into the room. Pushing myself to my feet, I studied the creature.

The snake was a shimmering purple with lifeless gray eyes (I guess if I lived in a maze of pain my eyes would look like that too), wider and taller than the height of me and too long to fit into the room. It focused on me, propelling more of its body into the room with a flick of its tail. I heard the repercussions of the force behind it, the crashing of stones. If I survived this then I'd have an easy way for the next couple of rooms; it sounded like the snake had leveled the walls. I slashed at it, wincing when my sword ricocheted with a shocking vibration. This was going to be much harder than I thought it would be.

I stabbed again, aiming for its eyes and missing as it dodged and snapped its fangs at me. I was forced to dive out of the way when it lunged, watching it take a chunk out of the other wall too. I noticed a tile with the X marking on it and slid under my reptilian friend, pushing it on the way across the floor. I hit the wall, scrambling to my feet and finding a niche to hold onto. The floor of the room crumbled and the snake pitched headfirst into the dark, body slithering after. A roar that froze my blood echoed out of the pit and I hurriedly crawled along the edge, one foot after the other. The snake's head landed in front of me at the doorway. It had been ripped clean off the body, with the eyes gouged out. I shivered with one last lingering glance at the pit, and walked into the next room.

Four walls had been flattened by the snake's quick change in direction, and I climbed across the rubble. I winced at the rough edges cutting into my palms and scraping my knees. The destroyed walls gave me an idea.

I scrambled up the tallest pile that I could find, until I got to the undestroyed section of bricks. I found tiny finger and toe holds in the bricks, wrapping my arms around the wall as I ascended. Bob followed me up, lighting the darkness. I expected to hit a ceiling at some point, but instead I found the top of the bricks. I pulled myself up, balancing on the flat surface. From where I stood I could see the entire maze spread out under me. I followed the wall that looked like it led to the center, wobbling and almost falling when an edge crumbled under my foot. I also ran into a couple of giant spiders that I beheaded easily with my sword; they weren't as quick as the snake. I crouched down when I heard voices beneath me, staring over the edge to the room below. "Shh," I hissed at Bob, who, despite not being a living thing, actually dimmed for me. I gave him a thumbs-up.

"We should go this way," I heard Luke say, and I grinned in relief. I had found them, and they were closer to the center than they probably thought they were.

"No, we should go right," Alex argued. "I'm the one who used to live here, so you should listen to me. If we go right, we'll find the center!"

"How do you know?" Luke snapped.

Alex struggled for words. "I just do!" I looked over the top of the labyrinth again, impressed. He was correct; if they went right, they would end up in the center. I swung my legs over the wall so that I was in a sitting position, and motioned for Bob to brighten again.

"I agree with Alex," I commented, listening to them bicker. That shut them up.

"Who goes there?" they both asked in commanding tones. I waved for Bob to go forward so that I could make sure that it was actually them and not a goblin.

"Are you guys holding hands?" I giggled when Bob illuminated them, especially their reddening cheeks.

"How did you get up there?" Luke frowned, dropping Alex's hand and rubbing the back of his neck awkwardly.

"I climbed," I said rolling my eyes. "Proving, yet again, that girls are smarter than guys."

"We were just coming to save you," Luke explained, ignoring my remark.

"You were going the wrong way," I observed. "If you started from that way," I pointed ahead of us, "then you passed through the center or went around it, and if you came from that way," I pointed behind us, "then you came from the same way as me and you should have gone in the other way to get to my room." Now they both looked embarrassed, running their fingers through their hair at the same time.

"We were going towards the center coming from that direction," Alex said, pointing behind us.

"In that case, congratulations because you're," I paused to count the rooms I saw, "about five doorways away." They high-fived each other. "Come on, I'll lead you." I stood back up, teetering on the edge before regaining my balance.

"We'll just come up," Luke countered, trying and failing to scale the wall. I smirked at them while they tried to give each other a boost up.

"I'm leaving," I called down to them, holding my arms out for balance and following the top of the bricks around the corner, towards the glowing center of the labyrinth.

"Fine," I heard them grumble as they hurried to catch up. In the last room, I climbed back down to the ground, choking with the effort of descending one handed. Luke wrapped me in a hug when I got down and I let out a shriek as he crushed my bad shoulder. He stepped away from me immediately, finally noticing that my arm was hanging weirdly.

"I can fix that," Alex offered, "but it's going to hurt like hell."

"I've already been through hell." I laughed weakly, and added, "and now I need both of my arms."

"Hold her hand," he directed Luke, who squeezed it lightly. I squeaked when I felt the pressure on my broken knuckle, and he almost let go.

"What did you do to this?" he gasped, looking at my swollen bloody hand that was turning purple.

"I punched my way through a wall," I explained, blushing. I started to tell them the story until Alex jammed my arm back into its socket and I fainted.

When I woke up, I could feel my arm again. I tested it out from where I was lying on the ground, and aside from the accustomed ache of it, it felt better. Luke helped me up carefully, then stood back before he could cause any more damage. I gave him a quick peck on the lips before turning to Alex. "What's in the center?" I asked, gesturing to the doorway that was emitting a blinding glow.

"Just be prepared," he advised. I nodded and tightened my grip on the sword. "Where's Sterling?" He frowned, his eyes guarded.

"She didn't want to come with me into the maze." I shrugged, and he nodded looking relieved.

"I don't like her, but she is my sister." He sighed when I shot him a questioning look.

"Ready?" I said, stepping forward towards the door.

"Ready," they chorused and we crossed the line together.

First it was cold. The bright white was all I could see, and it burned my eyes after being in the darkness for so long. I felt around me for Luke's hand and found it. He gave mine a reassuring squeeze.

"Find Alex," I yelled at him. The roar of the wind around us was too loud but he seemed to get the gist of it.

He nodded and searched for a little bit with his eyes squinted nearly shut, before finding another hand, hopefully belonging to Alex. I started to shiver against the wind that was blowing against us; the maze had taken away my feelings somehow, so that I forgot to be cold or hungry. The only thing I had felt was pure exhaustion, but the light was waking me up. I heard my stomach rumbling and hoped that I would either die or get out of hell soon.

I held my sword out in front of me and started to walk forward, hoping Luke would copy me. The farther in we went, the colder it got until it was unbearable. Then it became blisteringly hot and then everything went dark again. I felt the familiar rushing in my ears and we shot upwards, landing again in a carpeted room. I sat up, with the tingle of eyes on me. I looked around and saw Luke next to me, still asleep. Alex was on my other side and I did a quick scan of both of them to make sure that they were okay. "Well, Sleeping Beauty's awake at least," a voice observed from behind me. I braced myself for what was facing me and turned around. I burst out into hysterical laughing when I saw who Apollyon was. Too much betrayal had broken my brain.

"Hey, Mr. Jameson," I said calmly. He looked surprised at my reaction, but I was too tired to feel too bad about my principal being the devil, and honestly, we probably should have guessed since the entrance to hell was in a chemistry room.

"You're not even a little bit shocked?" He frowned. I started laughing again; this was the oddest possible conversation to be having with the angel of the Underworld while sitting in hell.

"Not really." I shrugged, pondering it for a second. "I think it was the brown eyes. Everyone in your evil family has brown eyes."

"Dad?" Alex said sleepily, and for a second Mr. Jameson's glare was diverted.

"Son." he nodded. "Thank you for your help."

"My help?" He looked around in horror.

"You can go now," Mr. Jameson said, waving his hand.

"No," Alex replied, staying where he was. Apollyon shrugged and glanced back at me.

"Thank you, Riley," he said, smiling at me. His teeth were white but inside his mouth was black, even his tongue. That probably should have been a tipoff too I guess, if I spent time staring inside my teachers' mouths.

"For," I prompted, dreading what he was about to say.

"Helping me with this." He gestured toward the ceiling where a crack was forming. "Blindly sacrificing yourself for your family was so," he pretended to wipe away a tear, "touching. I bet you didn't even realize that all of them are going to die now."

"Why?" Alex said, before I had a chance to.

"Your sister helped me too," he continued, speaking to Alex now.

"She knew that I needed Riley to help me get out of this place." He switched focus back to me and lowered his voice as if sharing a secret. "As nice as this place is, I really need to take a break, get some vitamin D."

"You're already free, aren't you?" I asked, thinking back to him in the forest and, well, every day at school.

"Heavens, no! I'm free to go into your school since your foolish ancestors built it on top of the gateway to my kingdom, but I had to use this body," he waved it over Mr. Jameson. "And I can go into the woods in my real body, but I have practically no power over there. But after your blood is spilled here, well, then I'll really be free. Every drop you've spilled from that disturbing display of destroying my wall to fighting bravely through that maze has loosened my bonds, you see." He waved to the crack again.

"Why me?" I said, hoping that we had been in the maze for at least a couple of days. If I could stall him until the end of the twelve days of Christmas then he'd have to wait until next year when I would hopefully be far, far away, or dead. Either way.

"You, my dear, have the purest soul in the universe," he said and smiled, licking his lips. "Which makes you my nemesis, which isn't a term we throw around here." He gave a delighted chuckle.

"I thought God was your nemesis," I said shaking my head.

"That's the problem with today's society," he said, clucking his tongue. "People have freewill now. They believe in so many different gods and Gods that there can't be one up there in heaven," he explained, pointing up. "Which means that I've had to settle for having a mortal as my enemy." He sighed, turning his gaze on me. "Shall we get this show on the road?"

"No thanks." I smiled, proud when my lips didn't shake from the urge to not throw up.

"I thought you'd say that," he said unhappily. He raised his arm, Darth Vader like, and I was slammed against the opposing wall. I felt a trickle of blood run down my face, but I caught it with my shirt before it could touch the ground. I couldn't take back the blood I had already shed, but at least I could postpone this guy's plan. He held his arm up again, looking disappointed. I was pinned against the wall now, unable to breathe. "I never said that you had to be alive for me to have your blood," he chuckled, brown eyes flashing.

"I've heard it helps though," I offered in a choked voice. I focused on the stream of magic coming from his fingertips, bending it with my mind until he let go of me, his fingers blistering. Soul be damned; I would stay in this place forever if it meant not ending the world. I closed my eyes, imagining Mr. Jameson against the other wall, hanging by his pants. Nothing happened.

"Damn it," I cried, trying again. I groaned when I realized why I couldn't do anything mean. I was the white magic here; I had to use happy thoughts when it came to actual people, even if I could use it on goblins. "Fine," I snapped to my magic. I turned back to Mr. Jameson, who was blowing on his fingers, and thought of an army of bunnies coming up from the earth and enveloping him in their cuteness. Sure enough, a fissure formed in the throne room and rabbits came pouring out, knocking him off his feet. He lit them on fire with a wave of his hand, and the smell of roasting flesh made me gag and throw up on his carpet. Heck yeah, hitting him where it hurts. I imagined a tsunami, sweeping through this room and extinguishing my poor bunnies, and ducked when I heard the roar of the tide. I built an air bubble around Luke, Alex, and me, and waited until I was sure that Mr. Jameson couldn't hold his breath any longer, then I got rid of the wave. Mr. Jameson was lying on his back, his hair covering his face. Black smoke began to billow out of his mouth, twisting upwards, then solidifying into Big Boy.

"I tried to go easy on you," he boomed, "but you didn't appreciate my human body, so now you can deal with me."

"That was easy?" I cried, throwing my hands up. "Fine, now you get to deal with me too, I guess."

"You can do it," Alex called from next to Luke. I remembered my vision of freezing my mom, and turned back to Apollyon. I closed my eyes, opening them when I heard the crackling of ice. It spiraled up his body in one long strip, spreading out in swirling sheets. He roared, unable to move, but that was cut off too when the ice covered his mouth.

"We have maybe five minutes," I told Alex, rushing over to them. He nodded in agreement. "Get out of here," I begged him, and his eyes flashed in anger.

"No, it's my dad and this is my fault."

"Did you know that this is why he wanted me as a sacrifice?" I asked him, studying his face carefully.

"I wouldn't have tried to kill you if I did," he said darkly.

"Good enough for me." I focused on making another golden cocoon for my boyfriend, which dissolved and spiraled upwards, through the ceiling and hopefully back to town. "Your turn," I said to Alex. I pointed all of my brainpower to him, and nothing happened.

"You can't do that for me, I belong in the underworld," he smirked. "I can leave whenever I want to if I'm alone. And I can go anywhere I want here."

"So do it," I said, listening to the groan of ice under stress.

"No," he said simply. Apollyon detonated my ice, sending out splinters. I shielded my face against them, but I could feel them bite into my arms and neck. The crack in the ceiling grew wider along with Apollyon's grin. "Why are you playing with her like this, Dad?" Alex cried, trying to clean up the blood on my arms. I pulled away and he withdrew his arm, looking hurt.

"Did someone fall in love up there?" Apollyon smiled mockingly. "It won't last, son. You belong here, and she belongs, well, dead." He brushed me aside with a lash of magic, but I was ready for it and caught the energy before it could hit me, throwing it back at him. I'm a fast learner. I felt the usual tug on my stomach, but this time it was stronger, making me retch like the first time. "Very nice, Miss Owens," he panted, getting up again. There was a smoking gash on his forehead but he was otherwise okay. I cursed under my breath.

"Go," I told Alex again, mentally begging him not to be here when his dad rose.

"Be a good boy," his dad agreed, waving his hand. In a puff of smoke (smoke seemed to be Apollyon's thing) Alex disappeared.

"Where did you send him?" I shouted, horrified.

"To his room," he said calmly. "Now, let's end this." He raised his arm, a bolt of energy engulfing his hand. I focused all my adrenaline into a small glowing ball, almost the size of Bob, letting it grow and shape. I watched Apollyon carefully, trying to time my attack. He flicked his fingers and I threw my magic straight into his. I was blown backwards from the impact, but I was smiling as I hit the wall. I slid down it, rubbing dust out of my eye. Apollyon was shrinking down to human size; the collision seemed to have paralyzed his magic briefly. I still felt the hum of mine in my arms and I shook them out, sending a field of flowers his way. They tied him down long enough for me to catch my breath, but when my ears stopped ringing he was free and he had a knife. "I'm proud of you, darling," he said, imitating my mom's voice. At least we knew where the Special K got their talent.

"Don't be creepy, darling," I replied, in her voice too. He may have actual magical powers, but I had called in at least thirty times to get myself out of school. He was no match for my laziness. He was caught off guard, which I used to send an army of Stay Puft Marshmallow Men his way. It worked for the Ghostbusters. He lit them on fire too, shrinking them down to regular marshmallow size.

"Stop fighting this, Riley," he said, still in my mom's voice.

"No," I said, in my own. "And you probably should have picked someone that I actually like to imitate." I started a cloud of hail over his head, (apparently pure people can control the weather too) each chunk of ice the size of my fist.

"Enough!" he bellowed, batting the cloud away with a burst of wind. Roots sprang out of the earth, gray and deadly looking. They wrapped themselves around my ankles, pulling until I was forced onto my knees. I stared defiantly up at the angel, who reached for my sword. "When your blood paints the earth red, I'll be free," he said, licking his lips. At least he didn't do *that* in my mom's voice. He swung the blade towards me, and when it hit my neck it bounced off. I smirked at his efforts, nearly going blind with the relief of not being dead. "Guess we're doing it the old way," he said happily, aiming his hands at me. He started muttering something under his breath, and his hands glowed with power.

"Stop," Alex commanded, dropping from the sky and landing next to me, but it was too late. Apollyon aimed and let the power go. It hit me square in the chest, the stream of energy being sucked out of my body entering his fingertips. "Stop!" Alex repeated, pushing me out of the way and taking the full brunt of his dad, already high on my energy. He collapsed, his body shriveling up as we watched.

"That's what happens when you don't listen to your parents," Apollyon told me, not even bothered by his son's death, aiming his hands back at me. Alex said he could go anywhere he wanted, and he came back for me. I felt the natural wave of guilt, but now it was intensified by anger.

"You killed your own son," I said quietly, holding down the disgusted rage in my stomach. I wasn't the biggest fan of Alex either, but he didn't deserve it. Not this.

"He should have listened to me." Apollyon shrugged, and I let go. The fury exploded out of me in waves, rippling over the throne room. I felt myself rising into the air, glowing with pure energy. Apollyon was knocked off his feet, hit again and again with white light. It ripped through his chest, bringing his smoky substance with it, overpowering the black. I launched another attack, the beams going into his mouth, which was open in a silent howl of pain. They filtered through him, pinpricks of light leaving through his pores, swelling until he was gone in a final blast of radiance. I landed, running over to Alex and stumbling when the last of my power left.

"Alex," I said, shaking his arm. He was cold and his skin was gray; his soul began to spiral in smoking circles from his mouth, moving towards heaven or at least purgatory, and his body crumbled to dust. My knees gave out and I passed out onto the floor next to what was left of him. The last thing that I remember was rising into the air, supported by invisible hands that looked like blurred sparks to my squinting eyes.

I woke up to someone shaking my arm. Luke was leaning over me; I discovered that I was back in the chemistry room when I opened my eyes. "Did you do it?" he asked. I nodded, my head throbbing in the dull sunlight. He hugged me tightly, burying his head in my hair. "I knew you could, Rye." He helped me stand up, supporting me when my knees wobbled. "Let's get you home." He had to carry me after a few staggering steps, and I nestled into his arms. He put me down when we reached my door and I actually had to knock since I had regained my substance.

"You're alive," my mom said when she opened the door.

I felt my pulse with a surprised smile. "Well, would you look at that," I cried, replacing my fingers with Luke's so he could feel my heartbeat too. "It's a miracle!"

"You have got a lot of explaining to do, not to mention the fact that no one can find Alex, which I assume was your doing, and you missed Christmas which was very inconsiderate of you considering that all your relatives, excuse me but where do you think you're going?" she yelled at me. I was already halfway up the stairs. I blew a kiss to Luke before shutting the door with a wave of my hand. "You will come down and say hello to all of your family members, Riley Owens, or so help me you will never see the light of day again!"

"I'm eighteen, Mom, you're not the boss of me." I smiled, and with another flick of my fingers I froze her feet to the tiles and her mouth shut. Then I locked my door and crawled under my covers and didn't wake up for the rest of the twelve days of Christmas.

Chapter Eighteen

oing back to school after Christmas break was admittedly a little bit like anarchy for the first couple of days. Since our school was destroyed, through no fault of any of the students, we had to continue our classes at the public school that was basically a private school anyway since it was still full of rich people. Eventually the town council pulled it together long enough to grant the board of Conlet Academy one of the abandoned mansions that was big enough to fit us all comfortably.

The town had lost about five hundred families who didn't feel like putting in the work of rebuilding Racheston and would rather move to the south of France or some other expensive place. Luke and Jess and I helped Sterling have a personal funeral for Alex after everything was over, because as much as we hated her, her brother was a hero. It was the first and last time that I ever saw Sterling cry. Then her family moved too, claiming that the town was "bad luck", but I got the feeling that Mrs. Sherton was just looking for her next supernatural sugar daddy. This left the social order in disrepair, as Sterling was at the top of her group of stereotypically rich and shallow friends, which left the rest of us rich and less shallow people un-bullied and un-dictated to. "They look so lost," Jess observed sympathetically, glancing at Sterling's meandering friends bouncing from group to group. "We should invite them to eat with us." I shot a look at Luke who patted my hand comfortingly.

"I've got this one," he muttered to me before launching into a long winded explanation of why we didn't mix with them while Sterling was here and why we shouldn't hang out with them now either. This led to a twenty-minute battle of good versus evil in which evil conquered all and Sterling's friends were not invited to sit with us. Thank god for high school, right?

THE END

About the Author

At the time of this book's publishing, Mary is finishing her senior year of high school in Fairfield, Connecticut, (where she grew up). When not writing at 2 a.m. or reading a book, (which is most of the time), Mary can be found dyeing her hair a creative color, hanging out with friends, or helping out anyone needing a hand. She also loves playing the flute in her school band and being outside, and really wants a dog so if you're reading this mom please get me a corgi. She sends thanks to her family and friends for all the support, and hopes you enjoy the book.

Author Contact:

https://www.facebook.com/profile.php?id=100007706748530

43996600R00093

Made in the USA
Middletown, DE
25 May 2017